Scion of the Dragon

Scion of the Dragon

C. K. SLORRA

C. K. Slorra, LLC

Scion of the Dragon

The characters and events in this book are fictional, and any resemblance to actual persons or events is coincidental.

Developmental Edit by Abigail Schopen

Copy Edit by R.J. Catlin

Interior Design by Alli Prince

Cover Art by James Meraki

Print ISBN: 979-8-9913221-0-2

Ebook ISBN: 979-8-9913221-1-9

Published in the United States of America by C.K. Slorra, LLC.

Printed in the United States of America

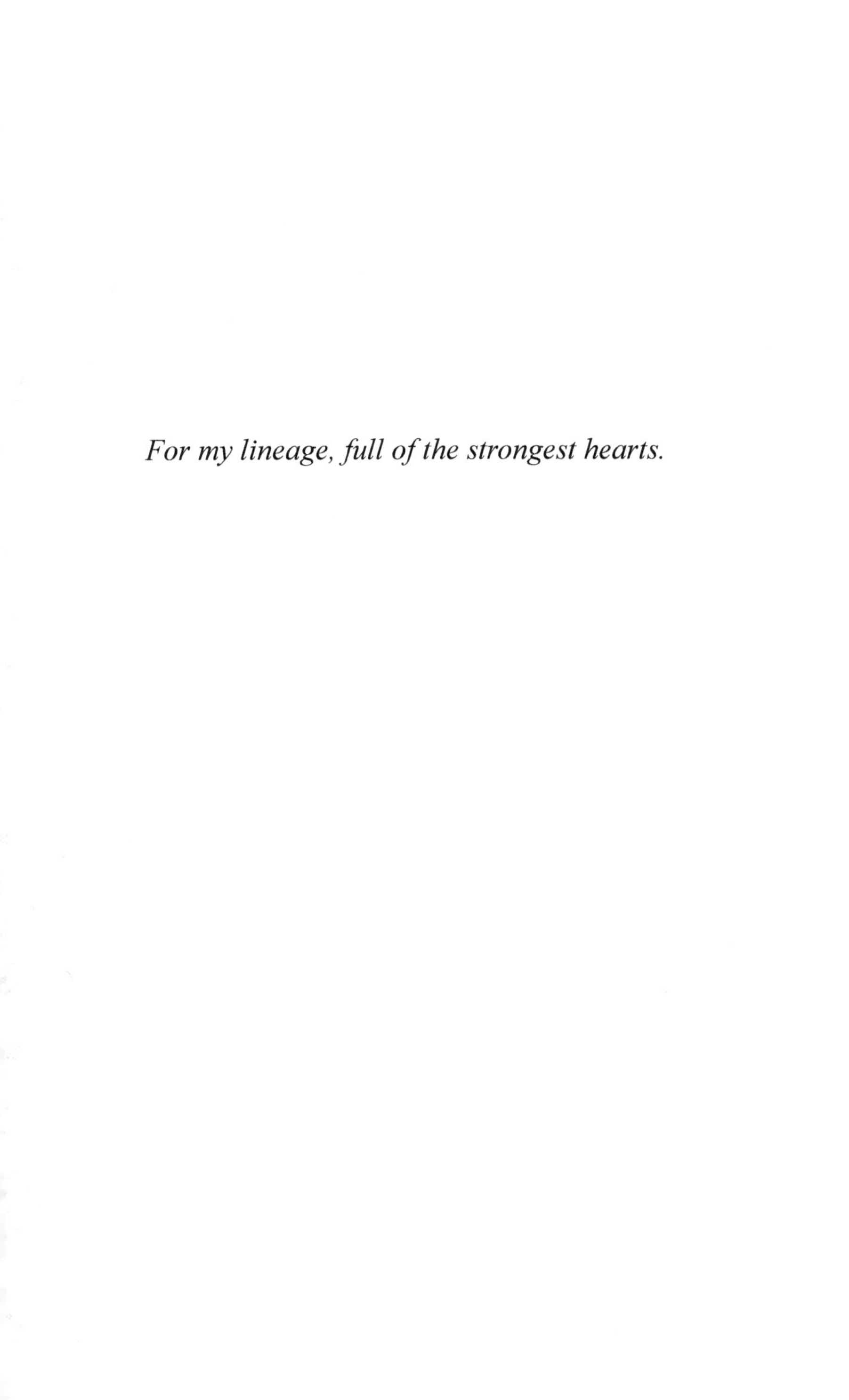

For my lineage, full of the strongest hearts.

LEGEND
THE CAPITAL
MAJOR CITY
MINOR CITY
DRAGON STRONGHOLDS
TIGER STRONGHOLDS
MONKEY STRONGHOLDS
THE BARREN TUNDRA
THE WEST
THE DURGA RANGE
PORT MIRE
THE DEAD PASS
JANGALA
THE SERPENT'S TEETH
MOSHUI WOOD
AGARWOOD
CAIFU
HONIN
THE CLIFFS OF SHIWA
THE YUAN TOBU SEA
YULKA BAY
THE CONGLIN ISLES
N
W
E
S
THE EMPIRE OF XINYUE

Seven Master Lineages

Master Kashvi   **The Qilin**   *Heir Zimo*

Unlike all the other master lineages, the Qilin has no offensive capabilities. Based off the mythological creature for which it is named, the art has mastered **healing** and defense. Thus, the Qilin is charged with the **emperor's health** and resides in the Marble Palace.

Master Hito   **The Dragon**   *Heir Sanav*

Though recently forsaken, the Dragon historically held the position of highest esteem among the martial lineages for its unstoppable nature. Emperors past charged the Dragon with **expansion**, but the last decade has held peace while the new emperor rises to his station.

Master Feiyu   **The Leopard**   *Heir Kirima*

A softer style, the Leopard art relies on speed and fluidity. Though numerically less than any other lineage, each of the Leopard's soldiers are trained to perfection. Their skills have been honed to **protect** the **emperor** and the capital of Xinyue, **Caifu**.

Master Kabir   **The Tiger**   *Heir Baihu*

Explosively powerful, the practitioners within the Tiger lineage have one purpose—to break and rend the opposition. Though historically charged with **border defense and supporting** the Dragon's **expansion** efforts, rumors suggest the tiger will be taking the next charge of expansion.

Seven Master Lineages

Master Isamu   **The Snake**   *Heir Shintaro*

This intangible art has earned its place among the other lineages through precision and strategy. While other lineages rely on war to give them purpose, the Snake only needs criminals; its charges are the **prisons** of Xinyue.

Master Rohak   **The Rhino**   *Heir Jai*

Creating soldiers capable of withstanding astonishing assaults to the body, the Rhino is at its best in the heat of **battle**. The years of peace have put a strain on the Rhino lineage most of all.

Master Patish   **The Monkey**   *Heir Mehnaz*

The Monkey's art is best described as rolling blunt force. It's hard to say whether their animal paradigm or their charge over the **seas** influenced the style more.

1

"I made it in time," I breathed as I passed through the hulking, bronze, capital gates along with dozens of visitors. With so few days to travel from the mountain fortress, Master Hito doubted I would arrive on time, but I was never one to fold before the cards were turned. After all, he had strict standards for his students, and a feeble heart would never make the cut.

The Xinyue Empire prided itself on the seven master lineages that each had a role in protecting the empire and growing its borders—and the Dragon stood above them all. At least, it did before its name was besmirched. I scanned the faces of thousands of people who owed their lives to the Dragon lineage, which had subdued many kingdoms.

As I let the river of people guide me onto the main road, I remembered why I hated this place. It wasn't the red terraced rooftops or the beggar children scattered at the edge of the alleys. It wasn't the people of Xinyue—I loved seeing them revel in the freedom I had helped create. It was how the capital's cobbled streets crawled with merchants and chaotic commerce. Every streetside vendor had their stalls packed with trinkets and paraphernalia. Patrons practically trampled each other for the first chance at haggling a necklace or a painting into their travel packs. Everyone and everything seemed to squeeze together in a way that took the breath out of my lungs.

I pulled to the side and pretended to survey wares of less populated stalls. In one vendor's stall, a cloth doll with black yarn for hair pressed against a wooden dragon moved as if alive. Every storefront had some version of paintings or figurines depicting the masters and their heirs.

One set of paintings stole my attention if only because of the way they twisted the heirs into grotesquely animalistic forms. The creature that was supposed to resemble me had a snaking neck with glistening gold scales creeping over my—its—skin. Wild amber slits replaced my upturned russet eyes. And were those claws for nails? As I drew in to get a closer look at the atrocity, the vendor snatched it back.

"Sorry, we aren't selling anything of the Dragon," he said, tossing the painting behind him. His face was blanched, and dark rings drooped beneath his hooded eyes. He stared at me without recognition as I stood stunned.

"Haven't you heard? It won't be a lineage after the festival. Pick a new lineage—maybe you'd like a Tiger painting? I have plenty of those."

His words cut like a sword, a familiar sting. I tried to say "no thank you" and turn toward the nearest alley, but I only managed the latter as fresh wounds reopened.

"We have done all we can do," Master Hito had said a fortnight ago. A tear had caught in the crow's feet at the edges of his eyes, warring with his rigid composure. He knew it was a lie. My master was tall, stern, and *powerful*. Nothing could truly stand in his way except his own principles. So, it had become my responsibility—my burden.

"Don't do this, Sanav," he had pleaded as the gravel in his voice grated against my heart.

My nostrils burned with my emotions. The same questions that had plagued me every step of the journey here now stung my mind. How could Master Hito say that to me? How could he expect me to stand by and watch everything he worked for disintegrate and fall between our fingers? He gave me my good name and now he expected me to curse his? Well, I wouldn't. A blaze had been lit inside of me and no one would snuff it out. My pledge on my life would be complete, and if he called me foolish for it then—

"Help!" A woman's shriek pierced beneath the shouts of the merchants on the main road. Her scream snapped me from my ruminations.

"I don't have time for distractions," I mumbled to myself, immediately feeling a stab of guilt. Did I want to become a person who ignored those in need? No, but if I was late, the other masters would be even less likely to hear my appeal.

"Please, someone help me!" Her screams strangled to silence in the next alley.

"Shut up!" a man snapped. "No one's coming."

"When did thieves get so bold?" I asked as I turned the corner.

"This is none of your business," a scraggly man warned, waving a knife as if he knew how to use it. Another rounder man held the woman by the neck against a stone wall that separated the masses from the next echelon of housing. His eyes fixed on her with a crooked grin, paying me no mind. The poor girl clawed helplessly at his hands, struggling for a breath.

I shook my head and strands of overgrown black hair caught in the wind, brushing my lashes. "Leave while I still allow it."

"Is that—" The words caught in the ragged man's throat as he stumbled back. "Is that the Dragon heir?"

"Sanav?" The bulbous man's walnut eyes grew to plates. He yanked the woman between us with a hand over her mouth and a knife to her throat. Her face dripped with tears as her nostrils flared. Light flitted over the mugger's face as a cloud yielded to the sun's rays.

"If you want to save her life, get lost."

I knew that voice– that face.

"The low life always suited you, Guo," I said.

"Not everyone got to go be spoiled in the mountains, Snot!" he sneered. Clearly, only one of us had grown up.

"If you recall, I have you to thank for throwing me into the Dragon's den, *old friend*."

Though qi flowed through all things as power, life, and influence, Guo's rigid stance showed no harnessing of it within him.

"Besides, you had your chance to prove yourself and I was better."

"Why you—" Guo flung the woman to the side and charged at me with a jagged dagger—a pathetic use of the meager energy he had harnessed. His sloppy charge was an insult to my training. I shifted to the side and struck either side of his hand with my palms, sending the dagger flying. My right fist collided with the underside of Guo's jaw. As my other fist circled toward his floating rib, I realized he was already unconscious. To think, someone like this once had held so much power over me.

I shot a warning glare to the other thug, who immediately bolted.

"Thank you, Heir," the woman said, wiping tears from her eyes. "How can I—"

I brushed past her, attention stolen by the time relentlessly ticking away. The capital guards could take her report and gratitude. I could only hope the masters had prattled amongst themselves long enough to still be there.

I reentered the main road, and finally, I could see the Agar Pagoda. It stood seven stories tall atop a great stone staircase. Each level had its own terraced roof all the way to the seventh peak. A crowd of people stood at the bottom, searching for a glimpse of one of the masters or their heirs. One of the children tugged the cuff of his father's sleeve and pointed at me.

"It's the Dragon heir!" he exclaimed, catching the attention of everyone around.

Great, I thought, as they swarmed, *I should have worn a cowl.* I struggled through the people, making frustratingly little headway.

"Where is the Dragon master?" one woman asked.

"Are the rumors true?" pried another.

"He's hiding!"

I could feel heat overtake my face as the accusation stabbed at my heart. Master Hito would *never* hide. He had always sacrificed for these people. Lungs alight with rage, I opened my mouth to roar, but a softer voice interjected from atop the steps.

"Have you no respect? Let the heir through," Kirima commanded from above. Sunspots speckled across her light skin which glowed like molten bronze. Even as the youngest heir, her master's esteem emanated from her, demanding respect.

I plodded up beside her and said, "I was fine, Kirima."

Her neatly pinned bun topped her head like a crown.

"You should not have come, San," she replied, entering the pagoda and pulling me to the right. Centuries old, the terraced masterpiece still smelled like sweet perfume. The weathered years had not so much as touched the aroma of the agarwood floors. To one side were doors to outer rooms, on the other side, a small wooden fence skirted the edge of a beautiful rock garden. Time seemed to freeze as I watched the frozen waves dancing in the sand around the rocks in perfect, circular patterns.

"It is the Festival of Heirs," I said. "This is precisely where I should be."

"Not anymore."

I crossed my arms and shook my head in disbelief. "I did not come to be lectured by the youngest heir."

She huffed, "Age does not make greatness."

That *would* be the favorite phrase of an heir just barely breaching twenty.

"But experience does," I said. I watched her movements flow in a rare and regal grace. Her war dress, threaded with golden armor, moved perfectly with her sway. There was a deadly fluidity in her dangerous gait.

"A few years of experience sets you beyond me?" She clicked her teeth. "But I digress. It is not right for you to be here. If it was, your master would have come."

The admonition stung. I wanted to argue, but Master Hito had said as much. Still, if I left now, the Dragon's demise would be assured. "I will have my lineage reinstated."

"Don't do this to yourself." Kirima's voice softened. "It is not your place to quarrel with the elders."

Her words only prodded the wealth of spite driving my actions. For a moment, we stood at an impasse. My vision tunneled on the stairs behind her. Kirima finally sighed and stepped to the side. If I had any friends left, she was a good one. Determined footfalls brought me from one floor to the next by way of a staircase that legends had ascended for eons. The windows let sunlight drift into the next floor to the most unfortunate of sights: the Snake heir.

"Ssso foolish," the Shintaro greeted with an oily smile.

"Shintaro, I have no time for this." In wisdom, I knew to ignore his antics. In anger…

"Ssso quick to complete your humiliation, Sssan?"

I stepped to him, but the vexing snake slipped to the side. "You should have stayed with your massster."

"I have the right to be here. I will prove the Dragon's worth," I said, reaching the next staircase.

"You have no rightsss, orphan of the conquered."

I feinted a lunge at him and felt the wind from his lungs escape. Shintaro hissed a laugh even as he retreated. Pest. He knew nothing of my people, no one did.

I paused at the top of the stairs before stepping onto the seventh floor. Under most circumstances, no one was permitted entrance without the approval of one of the masters. I had cause to ascend on my own, yet I felt exposed without Master Hito at my side. From the first moment I had stood, or rather collapsed, in the pagoda, my master had guided my steps. Only with his approval could I stand among the other masters on the final floor. It was sacred ground. I had his written approval. I just lacked his presence and I knew the other masters would make a spectacle of that fact.

The whitewashed walls were lined with ink paintings of heirs and intricate sculptures of the masters. The deeper I walked across the agarwood planks, the more recent the figures became until I stood face to face with Master Hito, shadowed by a much younger, ink version of myself. They chiseled him with stern creases and a dour expression. A faint chuckle puffed through my nose. He likely was in a dour mood having to sit and be sculpted. "What a waste of a fleeting commodity," I could almost hear him say.

Almost.

Turning, I knelt before the bamboo door to the inner sanctum. Strong voices reverberated from within, casting blessings on one of the heirs. Every moment fueled an ever-growing impatience in my gut. The moments crept by, like days spent perfecting a single step in a kata, our structured forms that taught anything from breathing to moving to striking and so much more.

"May the emperor's blessing carry you to destiny," came the final benediction from the Qilin master.

The door slid open, presenting the giant that was Jai. Though not the greatest of the heirs, the Rhino heir was the most impressive-looking.

"San, why have you come?" the Rhino master, Rohak, called beyond the doors.

With a respectful bow, I stood and entered. The dark-skinned speaker sat formally on his mat, feet folded under him, broad shoulders firmly set. In the center of the room, a pristine fighting mat lay untouched. I had only ever seen one master step onto the straw mat to challenge another; it was over in seconds. Surrounding the mat were rosewood columns inlaid with golden imagery of the foundational elements: fire, wood, metal, water, and earth. Between each column sat a pair of watching eyes—six of the master lineages.

Light descended on us from a lattice pattern on the roof. On days as perfect as these, the wooden panels were pulled back to open the four sides of the pagoda's peak to the underside of the roof. The glazed tiles remained, but the tiniest of pinpricks had been chiseled through them in a way that permitted light to pass and yet appeared flush to the eye. No room for spies, assassins, or arrows, only the casting of illumination on the inner chamber.

I dared to meet each of the masters' eyes. I sought their approval, but I would not grovel to get it. The Dragon lineage was one of strength and prowess, and that would never change. Each of the masters reacted in their own ways, but the way the Snake master, face sharp and thin, watched with an amused gleam unsettled me. Though heirs were never familial, he and his heir, Shintaro, shared spindly fingers and dagger-like eyes that prickled the back of my neck. Woe to those who saw the snake and thought him weak. Master Hito often reminded me it would be my responsibility to keep the Snake from straying.

"Lost to their intellect," he called them.

Unnerving as the Snake master might have been, his interest had been piqued. It was the Tiger, arms shredded with scars, who snarled and radiated animosity.

"I understand that my presence causes you discomfort. My lineage has been renounced and my rights with it. However, Master Hito has sent his endorsement to allow my participation in the competition of heirs if you would consider the Dragon for what it once was and may yet be again," I petitioned.

"An endorsement means nothing from a forsaken master," dismissed Master Kabir. As the second martial lineage, the Tiger had everything to gain from the fall of the Dragon. I had half a mind to outright accuse him, but I knew that would meaninglessly curl his whiskers.

"You will listen to my master's words," I dared. Sorrow and anger mixed, smothering my better judgment like thick tar. "Or have you forgotten how he saved you from the madman of the timberland?"

The Tiger master growled, "I will not listen to a hidden coward."

"As if he would hide from *you*."

"Sanav, mind yourself," Master Feiyu warned to my left. His ebony eyes were surrounded by soft, gently pressed features.

I dipped my head. The Leopard often acted as an intermediary in turbulent interactions, a commendable challenge. "My apologies, Master Feiyu."

"Your words were not against me."

I eyed Master Kabir resentfully. Locked in a fiery standoff, I emptily apologized, "Forgive me, Tiger master."

He only growled in response.

"Master Hito sought to avoid violating the emperor's wishes but believed in my right to take part in the competition of heirs. You will find his argument beneath his seal," I explained, bringing forth an envelope with Master Hito's seal, a dragon stamped into azure-colored wax.

"Your presence defiles this room as much as his," the hulking Rhino master said.

I bit my tongue before I got myself banished. They spoke of things they hardly understood. Even before the emperor forsook him, my master was misunderstood. They used to call him harsh and severe because of how he forced his subordinates to train, but in his rigor he showed more kindness than any. He ensured our safety not only through his perfection, but through ours also.

If I was honest, I had misunderstood him too. I had thought he resented me with as much as he had insisted I not come. But standing beneath such ridicule, and knowing it would only get worse if they accepted my appeal, I realized Master Hito was just trying to protect everyone with what little sway he had left. A knot formed in my throat threatening to strangle any more words. I hurried to finish the discourse.

"Even a forsaken lineage is granted a period to regain the emperor's favor, Master Rohak…" and Master Hito had waited six months too long to be restored.

"As if you *could* after your master's refusal," the Rhino master scoffed.

How dare they cast their scorn so easily. No one was as great nor as noble as Master Hito and yet they spoke as if they could call themselves superiors. I pressed, "You desecrate your own tradition if you deny me today."

The Rhino master puffed with anger, but I turned to the true judge in the room. She stood in front of the pillars directly across the straw mat. Her light frame seemed so free that I could swear her feet hovered above the wooden floor.

"Master Kashvi, as adopted kinship to the emperor, would you take this letter and consider my commission?"

All eyes turned to the woman with ivory skin. Her oval eyes hid behind blades of silky black hair. The Qilin, a one-horned creature of perfect benevolence, rose above the other lineages without any bloodshed. Though the lineage has no offensive capabilities, the strength of its heart and healing are unmatched. Thus, Master Kashvi and her heir held the highest honor of residing with the emperor.

Voice as smooth as honey, she asked, "You understand that even undefeated victory will not win the approval of the emperor, yes?"

"I understand. It is only the beginning of my… repayment," I carefully responded.

"Very well, I will see the letter," she said. Several of the masters spouted their grievances but she held a hand high and continued, "Each of the masters will be allowed to share their conviction on the matter. However, the young man speaks truthfully; he is within the time of recompense."

"Thank you, Master Kashvi." I bowed.

The Qilin master dismissed, "Leave us to deliberate. You will have an answer within the hour."

As soon as I walked out of the room, angry shouts pierced the air. Though indistinct, the muffled discord followed me to the floor beneath the masters.

I paced impatiently as the seconds ticked by. My heart pounded in my chest, like a gavel banging the beat of an unforgiving verdict. To ask for an answer within the hour was like asking to divert a major river in a day, and yet the wait felt like an eternity. I had to participate. I had to prove the emperor could not afford to forsake the Dragon—*my* lineage. Pride swelled in my chest. I dedicated my life to the greatest master lineage and thus to guarding the empire. No one dared challenge my master, so they sought to undermine his name. For what? He never envied the throne or else he would have taken it and no one could have stopped him.

On my life, they would recognize us again. He didn't deserve to disappear from history.

"With that look, I can't tell if you were denied or approved," Kirima mused from the descending stairway.

I started at her appearance. "I—neither. I await their verdict."

"Ah," she sighed. "That explains the intense glower."

"Did you need something, Kirima?"

"I thought *you* might," she said. Her silvery blue eyes scanned me with…something. Concern?

"Hm?" I raised an amused eyebrow. "Offering a shoulder to lean on?"

"Master Feiyu would hardly approve," she scoffed. "In truth, I thought it was only fair that you know the others intend to make an example of you."

"Oh?" I said, though I knew exactly what she meant.

"If even the great Dragon lineage can be cast aside, the empire is truly untouchable. Or so they will say," she replied, a note of regret in her tone. "You will accomplish nothing here."

She was right to say an example was being made of us. Master Hito described in painstaking detail what our futures held at the end of the time of recompense. Whereas only a handful of my people had been paraded and sold, the entirety of the Dragon lineage would be repainted in the empire as miscreants and every book that recorded the Dragon's glorious history would be burned. The executions that would follow were the least of my worries. Death was part of our lives as the protectors of Xinyue. What worried me most was how we would be remembered…or wouldn't.

My small tribe had long since been forgotten, and I feared that fate for my lineage most of all. A knife twisted in my heart. I couldn't remember my father's face, nor my mother's. I could search every book and ask every person in the empire, but I would never find a picture or even a sentence describing them. Emptiness threatened to swallow me as I nearly lost myself searching for memories that had long since disappeared. To be forgotten is to never have mattered in the first place.

Master Hito raised me from filth and gave me a place among the stars. He stood through my anger and my tears, and he never lost his hope for me, even when the other masters scoffed at the urchin-turned-heir. I would sooner carve out my own heart than stand by, silently watching as his virtue was questioned and his name disgraced. I would do anything to keep his name in the books of legend. The lineages would allow the emperor to do as he pleased with whomever he pleased, but I wouldn't let him erase my master or my lineage.

I shook my head as my heart swelled into my throat. The more I thought, the sicker I felt. If I could just hold on to my anger, I didn't need anything else. I had set out to bring glory back to my master's name and it would be done.

"I would not have come to merely blow smoke," I said.

"Then to what end? What good could possibly come from this?" Kirima turned her head to the side, hiding a pained expression. It was true. If I failed, there would be no telling of the humiliation I would suffer until the others were 'escorted' to the capital.

"A complete victory cannot be overlooked, even by the emperor," I said.

She whistled with an eye roll, "You speak so lightly of defeating the heirs in battle. I should be offended."

"Be what you will," I replied with conviction, "but this is not about the prowess of heirs; it is about the survival of a lineage. The Dragon lineage will not die defeated."

"Without the Dragon master showing his face?"

"He will, when—"

We both froze as Master Feiyu materialized between us.

Kirima bowed her head to her master, a stray hair cascading in front of her face. I quickly ducked my head in a bow. Would I be sanctioned? Surely they could not deny me.

I could feel the Leopard master's dark eyes assessing me. Even as the weight of his contempt rested on my shoulders, the Leopard master spoke to Kirima.

"I expect my heir to follow the wishes of the emperor."

Despite the injustice of the accusation, I held my tongue. Kirima was the pinnacle of obedient nobility, but my defense would only disgrace her.

"Forgive my curiosity, Master," she apologized.

"And I expect a forsaken heir to mind his place within the capital," he said to me. "Even if he is permitted to stay."

My ears perked. "I have been sanctioned?"

"For the duration of the festival," he clarified, with an expression that was impossible to read. "Tread carefully, Dragonling."

"I will walk with all integrity," I promised, rising from my bow. Kirima turned in a way I couldn't explain any more than the stab of betrayal in my chest.

"You will find your provisions on the first floor. When the moon appears, the fireworks will begin on the palace steps. Do not be late," the master instructed sternly.

I bowed to the master and receded to the lowest level. Someone had plastered a Dragon insignia on the sleeping chamber, as if I needed direction. The room consisted of ceremonial robes folded to one side and a bedroll to the other. Light streamed from the open red-trimmed window. Even the wind could not rejuvenate my tired bones. Traveling from the mountain fortress had not been without strain.

Just as I sat on the bedroll, the entire room shook. I shot to my feet as a giant hand clamped the edge of my door and slung it open. It was a wonder the wooden floor upheld Jai.

"You should not have come," the Rhino heir declared between footfalls. Deep, intentional scars created lighter patterns across his umber feet. His flowing pants and velvet shirt held enough shiny bobbles to buoy him in the ocean.

"So I have been told and told again," I grumbled, evaluating my options. Among mere thieves, I was untouchable. Here, it was the esteemed lineages that sat atop the hierarchy. In skill, I knew I was superior to Jai, but fighting back would relinquish my official sanction. I dropped my pack in preparation.

"Leave."

"My presence is sanctioned, Jai. I'm staying."

The behemoth of a man looked around the humble sleeping quarters and scoffed, "Sanctioned…not safe."

I gritted my teeth and snuck a step toward the window. "Is that a threat?"

Jai slid the door shut in sync with the snapping sound of the window closing behind me. I stole a glance at the backlit woman on the other side—the Monkey heir. Mehnaz was a troublemaker, but I hadn't expected her to join the cruelty. I did expect the hissing laugh from the hall. Shintaro would take any chance to express his sadism, and Jai's simple standards pit us against each other. You were either in or out in Jai's beliefs. And I was out.

For the other two, this was merely an interesting spectacle. A lineage hadn't been forsaken since before the Tiger's rise centuries ago.

"Stupid Dragon," he said, looming closer.

"Cowards," I breathed, fighting the urge to back away.

"Cowards run," he said, "I see a coward in your stance."

What could I do? Jai was the perfect assailant for this circumstance. Though many thought of the Rhino art as impervious, it would have been more accurate to say it was unstoppable. I would need to become so mobile I could not be touched, an impossible task in a room that practically equaled Jai's wingspan. Yet my only option was to try.

With his first swing, I ducked low, baiting the kick that inevitably came. His leg swung over me as I hit the floor and rolled beneath. He pulled his foot back to stomp, but I was already around the other side.

With a grunt, Jai flung his fist back at me. I slipped to the right, riding the wind of his strike behind him again. I stayed my hand from the series of potential blows along his ribs and spine. He reversed directions, swinging his elbow back at me. I bobbed under and back up, right into the front side of his other elbow.

I hardly felt the collision until my head hit the ground and three Jais danced above me. He stomped at my chest, but I had enough sense to move. I tried to roll all the way to my feet, but he was on me in a moment. His knee weighed on my chest like an anchor, sinking deeper and deeper until all air had left my lungs. I clenched my fist and gritted my teeth.

Master Hito warned me this would happen. He told me I would be better off abandoning his legacy and joining another militia, but I would have our dignity restored even at the cost of my life. I signed up to die for him, not the other way around and yet he asked me to forsake him like the rest. How could he expect me to abandon him—to run away and accept being orphaned again?

I forced what air I could into my lower lungs. Jai put a quick stop to that with a hand around my throat.

Don't fight back, I reminded myself over and over. Our eyes locked onto each other. His earthy brown eyes were unwavering though they narrowed like my vision. Just as my vision grew black, Jai lifted me by the throat and threw me into the wall. I gasped for air as a fist crashed into my gut. I bent over wheezing. He grabbed the back of my neck and threw me the rest of the way down. I hit the ground with a resounding thud. Jai stamped a heel into my side. I would have been insulted by the lackluster technique he was using to batter me if it wasn't serving his purpose perfectly. Every fiber in me burned for action. I could get up and make it all stop with one well-placed punch. Another kick crunched into my side, rolling me onto my back.

"Don't get lost in the moment," Master Hito had instructed time and time again. I had to endure until the matches began.

My door snapped open.

"Get out," Jai barked.

"You should be finished by now. Do you wish to taint yourself with his presence?" a blurry young man spoke with regal poise. Only one person could look so arrogant without even being in focus. I blinked away the haze to focus on my contemporary in white robes.

"He won't fight back," Jai complained bitterly.

"Did you expect him to in his position?"

Jai said, "I would not grovel."

"I'm not groveling," I groaned, stumbling to my feet before the lumbering giant and tawny beige warrior. "Do you wish to try your hand at forcing me to surrender, Baihu?"

"You would have to fall further than disgrace to surrender. Regrettably, your path has been cemented by your master's choices," the Tiger heir replied, coursing his hand through pompadour hair and rolling his gray eyes.

"Do you even know what he did to be discarded by those who revered him? Did anyone question it?" I fumed.

"It does not matter. No one questions the emperor—not even the great Dragon," he said.

"It doesn't matter?" I cried. "He served more faithfully than any master!"

"I will finish this," Baihu dismissed Jai, completely ignoring me. Jai nodded, content with the tradeoff. Mehnaz's shadow beyond the window also receded. Baihu turned back to me and his expression softened into sickening pity. "Perhaps you were not taught this in your homeland, but we are loyal to the emperor before anyone or anything else."

"When your master and lineage are trodden underfoot, then you can lecture me on loyalties," I spat back.

The princely heir sighed, "I will miss our matches."

Closing the distance in an instant, Baihu reached around and struck the back of my neck. I gritted my teeth and bobbed my head with the force just enough to lighten the blow. Even so, I crumpled to the ground. Consciousness slipped out of my reach with another blow to the side of my head.

"San, wake up!" A muffled voice buzzed in my dream.

I shot to my feet in defense to find the room empty and shadowed. My head pounded like a clanging gong as I shuffled to the window. My fears were realized as I saw the sky shaded a dusky blue. I threw the red ceremonial robe, hemmed with luxurious goldwork, over my traveling clothes. I had no time to waste and the heavy fabric hid the wrinkled clothes beneath. I was already out the front doors as I slipped my second arm through the sleeve.

Outside, the streets and alleys crawled with people trying to squirm closer to the palace. They would never reach sight of the palace steps, and neither would I if I joined their ranks. With a grumble, I took to the rooftops. Though I lacked the fine agility of a Leopard, gliding across glazed rooftops felt more like flying. Each gap I jumped brought life into my veins. I slid beneath a string of paper lanterns and hurdled a stray streamer, diving into a roll on the next roof.

The real issue presented itself at the sheer drop-off where the roofs ended and the grand market square began. I clung to a lightning rod and leaned over the edge, peering past the sea of people to glimpse my peers. As I searched for a clear way to them, I locked gazes with Kirima at the top of the palace steps. She slowly shook her head pessimistically. I beamed at a sparking idea.

I disappeared to the back of the roof and took a deep breath, forcing my qi into my legs. I bolted, sending tiles flying. I vaulted from the rod and shot like lightning over the crowd. As my descent began, I realized I wouldn't clear all of them.

I roared. One by one, people turned and pointed with gasps. The people at the edge of the crowd cleared a bubble for my thunderous landing which cracked the cobblestone. Even the throbbing in my head could not touch the invigoration I felt surrounded by awestruck citizens.

As I ascended the stairs, I exchanged glares with my abusers. Standing beside the lineage of the Leopard at the end of the line, the position of least authority, I turned and smiled at the conglomeration of imperial inhabitants.

"I wasn't aware the lineage of the Leopard had fallen so far," I said to Kirima.

Barely audible over the cheers, she said, "I am the unproven heir."

"Hardly," I said. After all, it was not she who had been placed at the end of the line.

Master Feiyu shot us a silencing glare, but nothing could quell the pride I felt representing the Dragon lineage despite their best efforts. Under a rain of colorful explosions, I flashed a hollow smile to the people. I held my head high, but I stood alone as hollowness ached in my chest.

Without Master Hito watching over me, was I even worthy to be counted as his heir? On my life, I would have his name restored in the Empire of Xinyue even if it meant resigning my place as heir when I returned to the fortress.

As the fireworks faded, the honored Tiger master stepped toward the people. His chiseled figure was striped with scars. A breeze passed over the people, silencing the clamor and gently blowing Master Kabir's unblemished silk robes.

"I wonder if anyone has ever seen Master Kabir smile," I whispered to the side.

"Says the Dragon's disciple," Kirima shot back.

"People of Xinyue," Master Kabir called out, crisp and steady. It should have been Master Hito speaking, just as it had been the decade before. "It is with great honor I initiate the beginning of the Festival of Heirs. Standing before you are the greatest warriors of this decade, some of whom have remained in this standing time and time again. Prove yourselves in the toil of the sun and cheer on your champions in the moonlight." He paused, directing the attention to his heir and those beyond. "Let the Festival of Heirs commence!"

Immediately, seven booms sounded behind the palace walls. A colorful display of animal-themed fireworks lit the sky as shouts flooded from the people, their hearts as light as the moon. My eyes shifted to the cracked stone steps, still devoid of life. The weight of the world rested on my shoulders, and yet it was a burden I dared not desert. I drew a breath and followed as each lineage trailed over a bridge across a moat into the palace courtyard.

Beyond the iron drawbridge and past the second wall, lanterns danced in the fluttering wind. The lineages slowed to a stop and waited for the cheers to recede as the masses found their way to their festivities within the city. In the shadow of the Marble Palace, the Rhino master stepped toward me.

"You mock the festival," Master Rohak accused, leaving room for his compatriots to join.

"Have you forgotten that this festival harvested you?" Master Kabir dripped bitterness.

"I would *never* mock the Festival of Heirs," I defended sharply.

"I specifically instructed you to arrive *before* the moon appeared," Master Feiyu said.

"Sss-certainly he would have had he not been obstructed," Shintaro spoke, letting the rest be configured by his gaze to the other heirs.

My knuckles turned white. "I don't need the protection of an instigator."

"Who?" Master Kashvi demanded, offense in her posture.

"Who knows? I mind my businesss," he replied, slithering back to his lithe master's side.

As eyes trained on me, I shook my head. It didn't matter what I said. What happened had happened, and I needed no protection.

"It will be avenged on the mat," I said.

Besides, whatever possessed Shintaro to defend me would not extend to supporting an allegation. All but the Qilin seemed satisfied, even relieved, to let the conversation subside. She approached intently. I stared back not in defiance but in resignation. I knew the fate I sealed for myself when I walked into the capital and I had nothing to fear from a lineage that could do no harm. She could, however, relinquish whatever she pleased.

Her hand hovered and then grasped my shoulder. Heat flashed over my whole body, swelling where I had been most injured. I gasped as the pain spiked in my bruised rib cage. I knelt and dripped sweat while I waited for the healing to pass.

"Tread carefully, Dragonling," Master Kashvi warned. "The emperor has declared that he will only hear Master Hito's request if you are victorious without the Qilin's touch between the battles to come."

"So it will be," I replied, getting my feet under me again. My rivals scoffed, but it was a small handicap in the face of an impossible task. Had I been free to fight back when they had attacked, I would not have needed the healing.

She beckoned her heir. "For tonight, remain here; your healing is not yet finished. Zimo will lead you to your accommodations."

"My things are still at the pagoda," I said.

She cast a maternal glare. "Master Feiyu can protect your possessions."

It was a kind precaution, but I didn't want to leave my pack for anyone to take. Still, it would be foolish to return to my assailants' reach before I was protected by competition regulations.

After all the lineages paraded themselves back to the grand pagoda, I followed Kashvi's heir past hedges, around rock gardens, and through endless vine arches until we reached a meditation hut. The shrubbery was masterfully tended and breathtakingly beautiful beneath the gentle, flickering torchlight. Leaves reflected hints of soft light and nearly every turn exactly replicated the last. Navigating the maze would be impossible without a guide.

"Is it not disgraceful for me to be within the palace walls?" I asked.

Zimo spoke as softly as a lullaby, "As far as I see, you have found yourself the victim of others' decisions."

"I am not a victim." I closed my eyes, then breathed an apology. Zimo more than doubled my age, but I often forgot to treat him as an elder. His lack of scarring and wear from the sun made him appear ageless.

Zimo smiled gently. "Your desperation can serve you faithfully, but it may also lead you to a woeful solitude."

"I cannot deny that," I sighed as he left me to the quiet night air. Solitude was the only guarantee in my life.

I rubbed my eyes and leaned against the wall. I was too tired to train and too awake to sleep.

"Busy?" Master Feiyu's voice asked.

"Wh—" I started, my hands springing to a position ready for a fight.

"Be still, I only came to check on you," he said. Seeing the Leopard master crouched in the window to my left, I let out a long, agitated breath. One hand clutched the window frame above him while the other folded over his knee.

"Did you follow me?" I was as much exasperated with his ability to surprise me as I was that he disturbed my peace…if you could call it that. "How do you expect to get out of this maze?"

"Didn't you notice every hedge is the same?"

"Yes, that's why it is so hard—" I stopped mid-sentence and snapped my mouth closed. Sometimes, I would seem far brighter if I knew when to be quiet. Every hedge was the same. That only gave it the appearance of a maze. It was a pattern, not a puzzle. That's how the others navigated it so easily. It would take some visualization, but the paths were simple if you realized they were all identical.

An irritating smile grew on his lips and then slipped away. He took in a slow breath, flickering out of sight and back in. "Kirima told me what happened on our way back to the pago-da… Are you well?"

"Don't worry about me. I have my sanction."

"That is not enough for everyone."

"Yes, I noticed." I subconsciously rubbed my aching side.

Master Kashvi could have used her full abilities to bring me back to health, but she chose not to. It was humiliating to be considered a trespasser even by the kindest lineage.

"You must be cautious in the days to come."

"Shouldn't you be watching my pack?" I deflected.

A breeze howled through the window, whipping his pitch-black hair into the room. He flickered and reappeared as if nothing about him had been disturbed. Only a few strands of hair were ruffled, the same ones that always refused to comply. The Leopard master futilely stroked them along the same path the rest of his hair followed.

"Kirima will keep a close eye on it," he assured me and continued. "You need to be careful. What Master Hito has done—"

"Don't lecture me," I snapped. "He didn't *do* anything wrong."

"Regardless," the Leopard master said, "there are those who think he did."

"I don't care what they think!"

"If that were true you wouldn't be here," he pressed, a crease forming between his eyebrows as they dropped into each other. "Hito is my oldest friend; I want this restoration as much as you do."

I finally barked, "Would you leave me alone?!"

No one wanted this more than I did. No one understood how much I *needed* to restore the Dragon's name. It was insulting to even suggest he cared a fraction as much as I did. If he cared, he would have been there when my master needed him. He *used* to be Master Hito's friend but when the emperor spoke, he adhered.

Master Feiyu stared with inscrutable, unblinking eyes. A moment passed where I wondered if he was anything more than a statue.

And then he vanished.

How dare he act like he had any right to offer me guidance. I knew my path and the thistles that stood in my way. I knew it would be easier to let the resentment, determination, and conviction go. I could return defeated, run away, and find a place in another militia. It even seemed wise in the stillness of the night. Yet who would I be if I forsook my master's lineage and the pledge I made to him? I would be worse than those who once called him a friend.

# 4

Inside the quaint hut, I sank into a meditative stance. The cool breeze rustled through the open window, bringing life into the otherwise still room. As my thoughts drifted, I hedged them back to the goal.

Perfection. I had to be perfect.

I had to imagine myself perfectly facing my peers. I floated from forms, to stances, to locks, to strikes, to sweeps—

"Don't forget your mindset," a memory of Master Hito from the last festival reminded me.

"My mind is focused," I muttered, sending the memory away.

I had dedicated every waking moment to mastery, as had those standing in my way. Most heirs had been training years longer than I had, but I knew myself and my history. I trained more ardently than any and it showed in combat. They came from nobility and that constrained them. I came from nothing, and that set me free to think only of my master and his teachings. The Dragon was all I would ever have, and it was all I ever wanted.

"This is pointless," Master Hito had said, "San, give it a rest. Let us ensure the Dragon lineage passes nobly, without vain strife."

"There is nothing noble about ignominy!" I snapped at the remembrance. I rubbed my eyes and took a steadying breath. "Let it pass," I reminded myself.

"Don't pretend," the hazy, yet audible voice jostled in my ears.

Something wrenched in my gut. My hands reached to either side as I searched this way and that. I took a breath and focused on what I could see…hear…smell…feel… Nothing moved, save the summer wind brushing the foliage that coated the outer walls. Whether paranoia or delusion, I could swear something was watching. The hairs on the back of my neck stood electrified.

"Show yourself," I called out, uncertainty betraying my voice. "Master Feiyu?"

The wind quieted so that all I heard was my own breath. Seconds ticked by like punishing minutes. Just as I relinquished my stance, an arrow shot through the window, zinging past my ear. I dropped beneath another bolt as a black-cloaked assassin flew through the window. Continuing my roll, I narrowly evaded the biting blades anchored on the assassin's bow. Some assassins added blades to the front of their bows in case they were pinned into close combat. This one leapt eagerly into melee.

"Are you mad? This is the emperor's grounds!"

The assailant drew and shot an arrow dripping at the tip.

Poison. Dastardly outlaw.

I dodged diagonally, shrinking the distance between us. The thin figure in front of me grabbed her bow with two hands and pushed the protruding daggers toward me as I charged at her. I bent beneath the blades and kicked at the closest knee. It popped cleanly out of the socket.

"Ah—!" A woman's scream came from the figure. She clamped down her cry as she clawed the knee back into place.

Her breaths were quick and strident as she scanned me from head to toe. I circled out of the bow's reach, kicking around into the side of her bow. Rather than break, the bow flew across the room, sticking into the wall with a resounding thud.

"Submit," I commanded.

"As if," she bit back, fire in her amber eyes.

"If you crave death," I replied coolly, "so be it."

The assassin stood warily as I waited. I had nothing to fear from a defanged stray and much to gain by watching. With enough attention to detail, I had a chance to learn who had sent the rogue.

She extended both hands, closing them into fists with one protruding knuckle. It was like my dragon's fist, but slightly different. It was odd, but it told me precision was her strategy rather than force. With one movement, she disintegrated the gap between us. I batted the first fist to the side and struck up at the second, putting my fist perfectly in line to crash through her skull had she not sunk and swiveled a sweep at my legs.

I leapt back, assessing her style. It swooped like a Leopard, and crashed like a Tiger, with a fist reminiscent of a Dragon. What was she?

"You should have stayed in your nest, Dragonling."

"Empty words from an injured miscreant," I said.

"Do I look injured?" she asked, descending on me with a flurry of strikes.

Try as she might to hide it, there was no mistaking her knee had been compromised. Even as she advanced, her resolve shook. I kicked at her injury and she jumped back. She whispered a curse, looking longingly at the window behind me.

"Who sent you?"

"No one sends Lera the Manslayer; I came of my own accord."

Unconvinced, I pressed, "No use lying now that you've met your end—who paid you?"

There was no response aside from a burning glare. She readied herself, raising those odd fists. I seethed at her refusal to accept defeat. I lunged, punching with one fist while the other hid behind the first strike. She reached to block my hand and I smiled.

I snatched the clothing draped beneath her arms and yanked her into my fist. I blunted the impact as it stuck her ribcage. I couldn't kill her yet; I still had questions. I heard a mechanical *CLICK* and a dagger shot from her wrist.

The blade sunk painfully into my forearm.

With surprise on her side, she pressed forward, slashing and stabbing with the dagger as we danced in a circle. I blocked and guided her wild slashes. With my hand, I parried at her hand, wrist, elbow, all the way until I could plant two fingers in the front of her shoulder. I dug beneath the skin and gripped the tense cord attached to her boney joint. I ripped the tendon mercilessly from the joint.

She screeched as the arm went limp and the knife clattered to the floor. She fell into the wall behind her, clutching at her shoulder beneath the layers of cloth. Her face was hidden by dark rags, but her eyes winced and twitched in agony.

I straightened and began, "Are you ready to—"

A blade zinged toward my eye. I snatched the sleek dagger just before it reached my eye. I flung it aside.

She had vanished, along with the bow that proved an assassin had come calling. I ran outside to chase, but it was as if the wind itself whisked her away.

"Sir!" a palace guard yelled on his approach with two others, "We heard a scream."

"Did it sound like me?!" Blood dripped from my fingertips. How could I let myself be injured the day before the competition of heirs? Every muscle in my body tensed, begging to be unleashed upon my foe.

"N-no sir," the armored swordsman replied, trembling, "but it came from this direction."

"I'm fine."

The guards' gaze sunk to my hand, slick and red.

"I said, I'm fine." I turned and slammed the door, bolting it and the window shut with the arrows that remained.

As for my hand, my sleeve would have to wrap the laceration. I was fortunate the assassin hadn't poisoned the dagger. Were her injuries ever to heal, she would surely not repeat the mistake.

I huffed to myself. How could I let her escape? I should have known she was pivoting toward the window. More insufferable, how did she vanish with the bow? Now I had no proof.

The puzzle ruminated in my thoughts until they slipped into dreams of blind dragons fighting demons with poisonous spit. Ever since I left the fortress, my dreams had grown vivid and confusing, teasing me by mixing reality with fiction just enough that neither made any sense.

When I awoke, the moon still lingered to fight against the sun's conquering light. I watched, entranced by the battle as I slowly unwrapped my hand to avoid any sign of weakness. As the moon finally succumbed, I took a heavy breath. It would rise again, gracing all with a softer luminescence.

"Heir, sir," a palace guard called beyond the door. "Master Kashvi would see you at the gate."

I wrenched the bolts from the door and followed the guard through the winding garden. Even knowing I crippled the assailant, my eyes and ears remained alert. Finding another assassin as skilled, would be a trying task for whoever hired this "Lera the Manslayer."

"San," Master Kashvi greeted, placing a hand on my shoulder. I cringed as heat unexpectedly seared my hand. Her head tipped ever so slightly. "So, it was true."

I eyed her cautiously. For all I knew, she could have lured me to be assassinated quietly in the emperor's grounds. The Qilin could not harm, but it might hire another to do so. Besides, what was I to say? An assassin made her way into the palace grounds and attacked me? It sounded mad. If the moat was not challenging enough, the guards of the grounds were highly trained watchmen, though not martially as adept as the lineages. "A foolish accident."

"The night before the trials?" she asked, compassion in her weary eyes.

"Master Kashvi, please," I bowed my head. "All will be well."

A grieved smile rested on her lips as she said, "May it be."

I lifted my head and nodded.

"For now, a signet bearer awaits you beyond the walls."

I regarded the open gate suspiciously. I had not asked for a signet bearer and Master Hito instructed me not to drag anyone else into my foolish endeavors. Master Kashvi merely opened her hand to the passageway.

Straightening, I crossed the drawbridge to find this signet bearer. I passed the arching gateway and a filthy beggar child bold enough to sleep against the palace walls. The morning was bright with a pleasant breeze and the sound of thousands of people bustling about.

"Master San." The beggar folded over himself and touched his head to the ground.

"Don't call me that," I said. The boy was caked in mud and smeared with blood. I was not the only one who had a difficult night. "I am merely heir to the lineage."

"As you say," he said.

I glanced around, but found no soldier awaiting me in black uniform. The child lingered in the bow, waiting for alms.

"If you point me in the direction the signet bearer went, I will buy your breakfast."

"Um," the boy stammered, "I *am* the signet bearer, sir."

"Let me see." I snatched him by the collar and pulled him to his feet. Truly, a circular badge of the Dragon rested proudly on his chest. The shimmering bright red stitching contrasted his mud-brown uniform. "Who do you say sent you?"

"Master Hito, sir."

"Lies." I gripped the boy tighter and ground out, "He sent me alone."

"I am your loyal servant, Heir," he insisted, rifling in his pocket.

"My loyal servant?" I shoved him away. "Do you have a name, boy?"

"Xael," he absentmindedly answered, rummaging through a different pocket.

I scanned the area, noting a few pedestrians immediately gluing their eyes to the ground and pressing on toward their destinations. The people of Caifu kept up appearances but they were as nosy as the rest of the empire. They would not step in to mediate for a young boy, but they would spread rumors of the Dragon's fangs if I was not careful.

"Okay, Xael. What were your orders," I fished.

"Master Feiyu sent a golden eagle with a message for Master Hito. He feared for you," the boy explained, retrieving a letter out of a rubber pouch.

I told him to leave me alone, so he went to my master? I sizzled at the underhanded tactic.

"I was sent with orders to be your shadow, sir."

I took the paper, wrinkled but dry, unlike the rest of him.

He had been through hell, judging by the grime and scrapes. I slid my finger under the azure seal and unfolded it. As suspected, the letter was not from my master. Captain Chiyo of the Western Fortress wrote it, confirming Xael's claims. She received Master Feiyu's message and sent this child to serve at my side.

Unbelievable. If Master Hito wanted me to have an aid, did she not think he would have sent one at the onset? An all too familiar sadness returned uninvited, chilling my bones and carving a cavity in my chest. I was only permitted to come alone. None of our soldiers were to be mixed up in this. Master Hito made it painfully clear that it was my foolish eleventh hour effort, and my life alone was to be risked in such a reckless way.

I folded the letter into my now sleeveless robe. "Why would you have been sent? Why not a proper soldier?"

"I am a proper soldier," Xael huffed indignantly, puffing his chest. "The fastest, sir."

"Even in the mountain range, a horse is faster than a man."

"Nothing is faster than descending the Eastern Cliff," he claimed.

"Impossible." I waved him off. The Eastern Cliff face was sheer as smoothed jade, and what cracks existed held venomous inhabitants.

"It is possible!" he insisted, "I was trained in the ways of the Binturong."

"What is—" I stopped myself. What was I doing arguing with a child? If he claimed to be part of a minor lineage, so be it. It was no slight on me even if he was lying.

"Assuming you speak truthfully," I postulated, "sending you was wise."

Albeit disobedient.

"So, you will have me?" He perked up, interrupting my sentence.

I continued, "However, I am capable of protecting myself."

His nose wrinkled and he retorted, "Perhaps physically, but a witness discourages much villainy."

I said, "The heirs are not villains, Xael."

"Captain Chiyo's words, sir."

I huffed at the captain's presumption. She was even more stubborn than I. If I sent him back, she would send another until I relented. Besides, he looked exhausted. "You may stay, but you will act reputably."

"As you say, Heir." Xael bowed again. I turned and began down the central way. Right on my heels, the youth asked, "Um, where are we going?"

"I promised you a meal," I said.

5

Xael sat on a stool, flicking his eyes between his fidgeting fingers and my approach. As a boy, I had dreamed of eating at this cafe. It was nothing spectacular. The food was good, but nothing to write poetry about. The seats were simple, wooden stools placed inside a wooden fence, instead of walls and a roof and a waiter. No, there was nothing particularly grand about this establishment except the satisfaction of a little boy who used to sweep the streets outside and salivate over the aroma of fresh food cooking just a stone's throw away.

No sooner had I handed Xael a steaming bowl then a mouthful of rice disappeared. As the youth scarfed down steamed pork buns and milk, I found myself lecturing, "It is most important to give thanks for what is provided."

"'Ank 'ou," Xael said, shoving a second bun into his empty cheek. I smacked the back of his head and popped both buns back into his bowl. Several patrons gawked at the regurgitation. "I said thank you!" he protested.

"Thanks is given in more than words," I said. "You show true gratitude when you savor the gift."

Xael's head cocked in confusion. "You want me to slow you down…to thank you?"

Amusement filled my face. "Not necessarily me. 'In everything, there exists an obvious answer and a greater insight.'" I don't know how many times Master Hito spoke those words to me along with some reprimand about being single-minded.

"The cook?" he guessed again. I shook my head, grabbing a clump of breakfast rice with my chopsticks. His brow furrowed as he watched someone else pay for their meal with imperial coins. "The emperor?"

"No, although some say so," I said at a lower volume. His face twisted in confusion, but hunger won and he took another bite, chewed, and swallowed. I could see the youth in his rounded features even covered in mud. Had this boy really come overnight?

With our stomachs sated, I led the way to the old healer Master Hito frequented in my early days of training. I could only hope he would still treat Xael even with my marred standing.

As I filtered through the crowds, a piece of me reminisced on my humble beginnings sweeping the streets of Caifu, and how the

Festival of Heirs had changed my life forever. Yet, another part felt the chasm of differences that separated me from the sea of citizens. For most, the festival would come and go in a week; for me, it was my last chance.

I veered into the back alleys, as more and more people swarmed market stalls. Even after all these years, I seamlessly navigated the maze.

As I entered the L-shaped clinic, nostalgic smells tugged me back to childhood. Scents of healing and a stoked fire heating the sauna just one room over. The warmth filtered through the thick rug used as a curtain to separate the entrance from the healing room. Tiles patterned the floor with white and gold, colors of health and prosperity.

At the counter, Pochi's head twitched toward me. His acute hearing made up for the mist covering his eyes.

"Dragon heir," he rasped, his ears tracking my steps. "Are you well?"

With a small dip, I answered, "No need to be concerned, Pochi."

"I will be the judge of that," he said, cracking his knuckles. He shuffled on the smooth, tiled floor.

"Po—"

"Tch" he held a finger to my lips, earning a snicker from the boy behind me. Pochi stopped, his cloudy eyes gazing right through me. "Who's this?"

"My signet bearer suffered many scrapes to get here overnight," I said. I pivoted to open the path to him. Pochi grabbed my arm and shuffled to the boy who was even shorter than the shrunken old man.

"Ah, let me see," he said.

Xael's eyes widened like a caught hare, frozen in fear. I shoved him the rest of the way toward the healer. Pochi felt the air until his hand landed on the boy's sweat-slicked hair.

"Oh," he said, feeling down his arms. The man pulled his hands back and rubbed the dirt between two fingers. "He will need an herbal bath first."

Xael started in protest, "Um, sir, I'm supposed to—"

"Remember the condition on which you are permitted to stay," I warned. Xael let out a dramatic huff as Pochi called for his apprentice. A boy not much older than Xael emerged from a curtain door. He sheepishly opened his hand to the inner room. With another grunt and a huff for good measure, Xael marched into the sauna room.

"Forgive his incivility. He's being raised by soldiers."

Pochi hummed. "An orphan?"

"I can only assume; he claims to have been part of a Binturong lineage," I replied.

Pochi stroked at his chin. "It must have been small; I have never heard of it."

"Neither have I, but I can't explain his ability to scale the Eastern Cliff without formal training." I passed five silver coins to the man. "This should cover the care."

"More than enough for young Hito's heir," he said, picking two coins for himself. Only an ancient elder could call Master Hito young.

"Come, come," he said, shuffling across the patterned tiles.

Paper lanterns hung unused across the threshold to the side chamber. Wooden panels creaked with age as Pochi found two jasper stones the color of turmeric. He lit a stick of eucalyptus and plopped it in a vase, its sweet, nostalgic aroma permeated the chamber. The sun filtered through the paper windows, casting light on charcoal drawings of ships and seas hung on the far wall.

"Pochi, may I ask how you and Master Hito came to know each other?" I asked, captivated by the drawings from a place beyond my imagination. The splash of waves against the ship sketched an adventurous life in stark contrast to the elder in front of me.

"Hito was a bustling young boy," Pochi said, shuffling past me. He paused at the wall, feeling the edge of the shelves lined with natural elixirs. Glass bottles of varying sizes and shapes contained herbs and remedies of all types. "He trained under me for a little while before the Dragon called."

"Trained to heal?" I asked, eyeing the square bottle Pochi pulled from the bottom shelf. Its murky contents careened from side to side.

A wistful smile lifted his alabaster eyes.

"You would have to ask him," he said cryptically. The desperation in me pled to know more of the life my master had lived before the Dragon, but before I could press further, Pochi popped the spongy cork from his concoction. A potent musk gripped my senses, stinging my nose and making my eyes water. I shook my head and rubbed my nose with a sniffle.

"What in the world—"

"Tch" he interrupted, snickering, "Trust me, this will give you stamina for the trials to come."

He dipped a finger into the dark liquid and wiped it across my forehead. Little granules of crushed herbs and silty paste rolled beneath his finger as he rubbed the mixture into my skin. A wave of vigor sparked my qi to life. I put a hand to my head as it settled over my body. My legs felt sturdier and my hands stronger. Pochi placed the elixir back on the shelf and took a seat on a cushion near the center of the room where the sunlight concentrated its warmth. I joined on a cushion across from him.

He took a deep, graveled breath. "You are tense, young San."

I gave a stoic nod. "It may be too dangerous for us to stay long. Last night, an assassin sought my blood."

"Oh?" Pochi's clouded eyes widened.

"Mhm." I debated whether to ask. "Did a woman come to you with a lame arm, injured knee, or shattered ribs?"

Pochi shook his head, an apology on his lips. "I'm sorry, young heir, I haven't seen those injuries today." As my mind sunk in thought, eyes tracing the intricate rug, he added, "If I do, I will send my runner."

"Thank you, Pochi. I will make sure your help to me is discreet, until the Dragon's name is restored."

Pochi smiled warmly. "Rumors come and go; I will always be proud to serve the Dragon lineage."

A glint of hope flashed in my heart. Not everyone had forgotten the lineage that ended wars and restored peace among the people. Xinyue would burn without our protection. So, who thought it could endure regardless of who its guardians were?

"How injured is the boy?" I asked, carefully hedging the concern from my voice.

"Like master, like student," he said. "His qi is fraying, but not irreparable. I will know more when I get the chance to examine his injuries."

"He's ready," the young apprentice called.

"Quiet down!" Pochi returned.

I jumped to help him up by the elbow as he struggled onto a knee. He grunted a thanks and rolled up his sleeves. A hint of an old, weather-worn tattoo peaked out from underneath one. Pochi quickly shuffled into the inner chamber where the sauna created a heavy blanket of steam that I could feel even beyond the thick curtain.

I settled back against a wall as I ruminated on the little information I had, searching for answers. To send an assassin was more than disdain for my presence. Assassins cleared the way for someone or something else. What was I thwarting and who sought my death?

I had made no headway toward an answer when Pochi returned with… Xael? The boy in front of me was even younger than the one I had brought. With the dirt removed and his scrapes cleaned, Xael's copper skin showed a youthful vitality. His cleanly cut, black hair swooped just above his zealous eyes as he fiddled with the new, traditional robes.

"Can I have my uniform back?" he asked as soon as he returned to my side, vulnerability showing in the way he tugged at the silk robes.

"Not until you have it cleaned," Pochi interjected. "The viper bites are the least of his injuries. His muscles need immediate rest. I did what I could to return the flow of qi, but he still needs a great deal of rest."

"What's qi?" Xael asked.

"Qi is the energy that flows through you, giving you power, strength, and vitality," Pochi calmly explained. "And yours is spent, young man."

Xael's eyebrows furrowed and his eyes bounced back and forth as if comparing two things in his mind.

"Which muscles are in need of rest?" I asked, wary of the added responsibility. Some groupings of muscle strained or healed easier than others—I needed to know how much attention Xael would require. My aspirations would wait for no one.

"All of them. It's as though, when one failed, another took its place. It appears the muscles in his forearms were the first to splinter, but his triceps somehow compensated until they too frayed. His biceps were the next to go, and it continues through his rotator cuff in his shoulder down his back, all the way to his calves. Even the tendons are worn thin," Pochi said, "It is a staggering sight."

It must have been excruciating to climb with such injuries while being attacked by vipers. What drove Xael to endure such pain for me?

"Thank you for taking care of him," I said. "Keep your head low until the Dragon is respected again."

The last thing I wanted was for Pochi to be pulled down with me. His healing would be invaluable, but I was prepared to walk this road alone for the sake of my master and those who stood at his defense.

"Young heir," Pochi pulled my attention. "Diligence and dedication are priceless qualities, but the Dragon must be the most careful to walk the path of justice lest it be swept up in darker ways."

I could see where Master Hito learned his cryptic proverbs from. It struck a sentimental chord in my gut, but I couldn't shelter such softness with the strain ahead, and so I shoved it out of my mind. What did he know of the Dragon's path anyway? To what did these "darker ways" allude? His advice would be different if he knew the path I had walked to get here. "Careful" was no longer a commodity I could indulge.

As soon as we exited, Xael said, "He's too high-strung. I'm fine, really."

I cupped the back of his neck and cinched his arm at the elbow, earning a sharp whimper. Tears formed at the edge of his wincing eyes as he withered in my grip.

"I can respect your determination, but do not lie to me," I admonished. "I would sooner have a coward than a liar at my side."

"Please," he said. His eyes burned with conviction and fear. I saw a reflection of my own desperation in him.

"I promise I'll be helpful; don't send me back."

"I intend to complete this alone, but you are in no shape to travel," I said, releasing him and turning down a smaller alley that could only just fit a pair of travelers side by side. "What path brought you here?"

"As I said, I scaled the—"

"Eastern Cliff, yes, I know your claim," I briskly interrupted. "But why did you come?"

The boy looked everywhere except at me. "Any of the men would have done what I did if they could have."

Unsatisfied with the lackluster response, I pressed, "Each for their own reasons, and yet you are the one standing at my side."

He shrugged as redness speckled his cheeks. "Captain Chiyo asked me to come, so I did."

For a bribe or promise most likely. Whatever it was, I sensed I was only pushing further from the truth with my badgering. Xael rubbed his arm as we walked in silence, the sound of our footsteps meeting our ears.

After several glances at me, he finally asked, "So, um, what's your plan?" He hastily added, "If I can ask."

"Hm. My plan is to retrieve my belongings from the pagoda."

"I mean your big plan, ya know, to redeem the lineage."

I passed a sideways glare at the boy. "I will prove our worth on the mats."

Xael quietly aired, "I saw someone bet a month's wages that you would declare a Worthy Trial."

Ah, a Worthy Trial. If only it was so simple. Whether a race or a headhunt, the emperor could ask anything as proof of loyalty. The problem was, I knew what he would ask for. The people didn't know what had already been sacrificed. Resentment burned beneath my skin remembering the emperor's request. No, a Worthy Trial was not enough.

I evaded, "Only a master can declare such."

"But you could declare it for the master," Xael pressed, undeterred.

I slapped a hand over his mouth. Xael's eyes widened and his body became inhumanly still. "Speak of this again, and I will send for your retrieval. The master will do as he sees fit for the Dragon's legacy."

Xael's shoulders pulled to his ears and his head bowed like a kicked puppy. After all the trouble he went through to arrive by this morning, he had to be exhausted, and I was henpecking his every move. Something stirred in my chest. Even if he was bribed into coming, any sane man would have quit after the first viper strike.

I sighed. "A Worthy Trial isn't bold enough. Think bigger." I instantly regretted saying it. There was only one thing bolder than a Worthy Trial.

"What's bolder than that?" Xael peeked out from his sullenness.

"Figure it out," I said. Perhaps he was too young to put it together.

A smile fought against my rigid focus. I would have to send Xael back before the tournament ended; it was selfish to even allow his presence considering the danger it placed him in.

We reentered Main Street on our last leg to the pagoda. It crawled with different kinds of people and clamored with all sorts of conversation. I casted a longing look to the rooftops, but Xael's injuries necessitated an easier path. I grumbled under my breath and began toward the pagoda. The people parted as I walked, though I could not say if it was because of my presence, status, or disrepute.

Xael puffed his way up the stairs to the Grand Pagoda. He hesitated at the entrance. The aura that flowed from the lineages' residence would make any sane man pause and inspect his worthiness to enter.

"You'll be fine," I said. Xael glanced up with quaking eyes. "You have earned your rest here."

We had hardly entered my room before Xael curled on the floor. He laid limp as a noodle with his back against the wall. His breath quietly rose and fell with an occasional twitch. Whatever a Binturong was, I could see how Xael might emulate one.

I knelt where I could watch the open window and door as I visualized the duels. A quiet breeze filtered through the room, bringing with it the sounds of a people unburdened by the upper echelon of society. With the Dragon lineage came the responsibility to become an unbreakable fortress and an unstoppable force.

"As the monsoons of summer, so are we," I could hear my master's teaching in his unmistakable, gravelly voice.

Xael slept so peacefully that I couldn't bring myself to wake him, but the night drew near, and I had yet to retrieve my pack from the Leopard master who was guarding it. I quietly moved to the door and lifted as I slid it to keep the bamboo from rubbing loudly against the agar flooring. I made my way to the inner path around the central rock garden, which was beautifully checkered in the daylight from slatted windows. The garden drew my breath with freshly tended designs. Line after line of sand perfectly traced the rocks, settling my soul. My circle came to a close at the first ascending staircase. As I stepped on the first stair, I heard Xael's feet thudding to catch up.

I could learn a thing or two from the Leopard's stillness.

"Go rest," I shooed.

"I feel much better," Xael said.

"Is that so," I questioned. He shrunk in place as I grabbed his arm. He spoke the truth. His muscles felt much more relaxed. Pochi was good, but that was quick even with his care. "Very well, you may come."

I climbed the first flight of stairs to the Leopard's domain. The walls were stained a deep red to accentuate the golden pedestals that held ancient relics.

"Wow!" Xael said with awestruck eyes. "Whose is that?"

He pointed to a curved sword, delicately placed on prongs above the sheath. Both were masterfully crafted with golden dragons dancing across pitch-black skies. The hilt's grip arced with red waves.

"The first Dragon master's katana," I answered, listening for Kirima or her master.

"What is this?" Xael asked, inspecting two war fans of unmatched craftsmanship. Their gold edges froze mid-drip over the silver fan blades like liquified rays of sun.

"That is the last of the Vermillion's war fans," Master Feiyu answered from somewhere. For such a quiet man, it seemed awfully showy to use his lineage's ability so openly. Even as he spoke, I could not spot him. "The burning bird's eternal sacrifice birthed our empire into the world."

"Who's there?" Xael leaped in front of me with a serrated knife.

I smacked it out of his hand and scolded, "That is the Leopard master."

The boy bowed at the waist, a barely audible whisper escaping his lips. "Master..."

"Was that directed to me or San?" the Leopard master asked,

stepping in front of Xael. He remained as rigid as a statue; even his chest refused the rise and fall of a breath.

I pulled Xael to my side and answered for him. "Forgive him, Master Feiyu. He is worn after answering your call."

The master's predatory gaze shifted to me, a silent threat passing through the space between us. His hands were tucked neatly behind his back as if keeping complete composure, but his eyes, black and bottomless, held a challenge I itched to return. Something had changed in him, and that sent jolts into my hands and fire into my lungs.

"The request I sent to Master Hito?" His resonance left an accusation in the air.

I pulled Xael all the way behind me with one arm, turning enough to put the other between the Leopard and my center mass, and returned, "Is there something you wish to say?"

He growled lightly. "Is there something you wish to explain?" He threw my pack at me. As the leather pack thudded into my chest, I snapped my hand over it, feeling the heft of the gargantuan gemstone inside. His scowl grew deeper. "Well, *Heir*?"

I swallowed, unwound the string, and opened the top of my traveling bag. I knew what I would find—what he had found. This was exactly why I didn't want to leave it overnight. Now he certainly thought I was a thief. I clenched my jaw and slipped my hand inside, rubbing around the smoothed bloodstone and feeling to the bottom. When my fingers reached the leather bottom, my breath caught. I fumbled through the random little supplies in a panic.

"You took it?" I snapped. He pulled a dark yet faded and perfectly frayed belt from behind his back. It had a new but browning hue of blood. He extended it as if daring me to try to snatch it back. I knew better than to enter a contest of speed with the Leopard. His posture showed no intent to relinquish his new possession. "Give back the belt."

"This is Master Hito's belt," he said.

"Not anymore," I finally blurted, water burning my eyes. "It's my belt now—my responsibility!"

Master Feiyu's face fell. He took a weighty step back. His hands fell limp to his sides, the belt flopping against the side of his leg. His expression shifted from anger, to disbelief, and finally to despondence. His eyes fixed on the belt quivering in his right hand.

"How?" he mouthed. "Did you…" The question hung in the air: did you kill him?

I opened my mouth to respond, but I had no wind in my lungs. My heart and mind disagreed on the answer. I looked at my own trembling hands. I gritted my teeth and reminded myself I was angry. I was furious. I was…all alone now. With one purpose, one person to avenge, and everyone to blame. If anyone had just—but they hadn't. In the end, he was alone, and now I was too.

"Master San," Xael tugged at my arm, "Are you ok?"

"I told you not to call me that," I snarled, looking daggers at him. Xael paled before me. Sweat glistened on his flushed face as it ducked into a bow without another word. I snapped my gaze back to Master Feiyu.

"Master Hito committed *seppuku* four nights ago under the waxing moon. I—" The words caught in my throat. "I was his second."

My cowardice wouldn't let me say that I dealt the final blow. To end his suffering, as the ritual said. My heart said differently. I killed him when I failed to change his mind. "After I buried him, I came here."

The Leopard still looked lost, his eyes flitting back and forth as he asked, "Why? Why come here?"

"To prove I have earned my place among the masters and restore the emperor's favor to Master Hito's name, as he deserved."

"He gave you a place among us; you already earned it," he said, restoring the clarity to his eyes and restructuring his posture. His grief carefully tucked itself behind noble poise.

"Do you think the masters or emperor would see it that way without a display?" I challenged, stepping to him.

He pressed the belt into my gut, the center of my qi. "It is not right for a master to humiliate heirs for show or celebrity."

I snatched Master Hito's belt from him. "It was not right for the masters to humiliate the greatest among them for vainglory."

He sighed heavily. "You have much to learn before you rise above your peers, San."

I fumed silently and headed for the stairs. He called after me, goading, "If you don't believe me, ask your signet bearer."

I descended to my meager lair, followed warily by Xael. Master Feiyu was just like the other masters. They preached glory, gallantry, and dignity but knew none of them. They were nothing more than frauds and cowards. I yanked my uniform from the pack. Much like the katana, it was black with golden trim that danced with dragons. I folded Master Hito's belt back into my bag and shoved both toward my signet bearer.

"If you lose this, you lose your life," I stated. Without the belt, my efforts here were wasted. Xael hesitantly approached. He grabbed the pack gingerly and I gripped his hand firmly to it. I must have looked ghastly for the fear to dilate his pupils so. "Do you understand?"

"Yes, Heir," he quietly said.

"Good," I said and clapped his shoulder.

I filled my lungs with all the air I could fit and released it in a puff of smoldering smoke. Master Feiyu thought Master Hito had abandoned me before he taught me the secrets of the Dragon art. No, he had not left me defenseless. This night would set the stage for my ascension. I grabbed my cloak and stepped toward the Hall of Lineages.

One by one, the heirs filed down the brick tunnel. Rows of torches lit the interior with an orange glow. It was my first time seeing the new Hall of Lineages. With the new construction, "hall" was a misnomer. The stonework was a traditional red, but the structure itself rose atop tunnels with cascading seating like the Western Coliseum Master Hito and I conquered years ago. The people of that land understood hierarchy, order, and respect. They vowed to join the empire if Master Hito and I could subdue their champion and his son in arena combat. Their sensibility earned respect in Xinyue and this coliseum was erected as a tribute to their honor. One day, I could be sure another champion would arise from their midst to make their place among the lineages, though I could only speculate which it would replace.

My shadow quietly asked, "Did you really fight a war in one of these?"

"Hm, more like ended one before it began," I said.

"Was it scary—facing the champion's son in the middle of thousands of people?"

I shook my head, "I knew by the way he walked that I would be victorious." The champion's son was just that, a champion given the name only by way of his father. Like all of the other heirs, nothing familial tied me to the Dragon lineage. I was chosen—a scion more than a formal heir.

"What if they hadn't honored their pact?"

I cracked my neck. "Then their coliseum would have made a fine mass grave."

"I heard it was huge," Xael said with a twinkle in his eye.

I smiled, remembering the massive structure. "They told me there is one even greater further west, across the water."

"Bigger than this?" His voice echoed in the massive tunnel.

Master Rohak called back, "Quiet, the ceremony is beginning."

I listened as crowds cheered for their champions. Master Kabir and Baihu of the Tiger strode forth first, followed by each of the others. The masters pulled to the left as the heirs continued straight into the center of the smooth, stone arena surrounded by thousands of citizens. I motioned for Xael to wait for me in the tunnel.

Someone had taken great care to keep the area devoid of dirt, even with the massive open archways behind the rows of clapping bystanders. As many people as had come, there would be tenfold listening outside for reporters to recount the match details. Those who made it inside were nobles and esteemed instructors from east to west, lining the seats with the finest linens and softest silks.

The Hall of Lineages glowed with brilliant torchlights made almost useless under the luminescence of the gibbous moon.

As Master Kashvi raised her hand, all noise ceased. The onlookers folded their legs beneath them and waited expectantly. The stillness accentuated the anticipation. Status among the lineages rested on this festival. What would be the hierarchy of the next generation?

With the voice of a tidal wave, Master Kashvi boomed, "Welcome to the grand display—the competition of heirs!" I wondered how her mild-mannered heir would ever take the mantle of speaker. "The emperor has decreed that to earn an audience with him, the Dragon heir must win every battle without the aid of the Qilin. In justice, he has also decreed that any heir who succumbs to the Dragon will join him in dishonor. They will immediately fall to the bottom of the seven echelons."

A hushed shock emanated from heirs and onlookers alike. My throat tightened at the thought. This was far from justice. Now the heirs would have more to lose than ever in the arena, and they would see it as my fault. Master Kabir padded up beside Master Kashvi and announced the order of matches. I would fight last all five nights.

Tonight, I was to face Kirima. I tried not to notice her shoulders fall. I tried not to let the guilt chip at my resolve. To win all five fights meant to spread the blight of my disgrace to all of the lineages. They would all have to succumb to any request of the emperor in order to be restored, and I knew how unreasonable those requests could be.

As the Snake and Monkey heirs took to the center, the crowd applauded their champions. Guilt churned in my gut. The Leopard master's scolding resounded in my mind. How could I subject my peers, people from whom I had learned, with whom I had bled and fought for the empire, to such disgrace? Kirima had so much to prove, but it wouldn't matter if she fell tonight.

Stop it, I chastised myself. They had earned this when they turned their backs on the Dragon lineage. I couldn't hesitate in these matches. I couldn't show mercy. If even an ounce of my being held pity, it would be the end of my campaign here.

Shintaro slithered his way to victory over Mehnaz with a chokehold after barely evading her crashing Monkey fists. Baihu nearly crippled Jai in a beastly display as clenching Tiger maws broke their way up the body. There was nothing inherently supernatural about Baihu's strength, but the ease with which he broke bones often made it seem so. Jai roared in pain as Master Kashvi set his knee, elbow, and shoulder in the right places.

This was it.

"For the master," Xael said. His bearing was sober but confident.

"Yes, victory for Master Hito," I pledged.

Kirima stepped with me into the light. Her uniform was a gentle reddish brown, with black trim that cleanly accentuated the deep-brown belt cinching it together. I watched lords and ladies watch each other for how they were "supposed" to react. No one knew whether to applaud their champion or shun the forsaken heir fighting among the master lineages. Scattered claps echoed. Their anxious anticipation covered the coliseum like the embers of a fire waiting to be stoked by a stiff breeze.

"I'm sorry, but I cannot let my lineage fall to ruins," Kirima whispered.

"Don't be, it isn't your choice," I replied, taking a stand as she continued across from me.

Jai's blood soaked into the stone in front of Kirima, deepening the red hue. The first blood in the new Hall of Lineages. It was cruel to put such a new heir in her position, but as with my master's plight, it was the emperor's tyranny, not mine. He demanded injustice. One day, she would be a frightful warrior, but with only a decade of training, she had much to learn.

We bowed, some say to each other, others say to the Giver of Strength. As the gong rang, Kirima inched over the blood-stained masonry, no doubt waiting for my assault. I inhaled and stepped into a light front stance. She pivoted to the side, wisely cautious and entirely focused.

With a sharp exhale, I tensed every muscle in my body and surged directly at her. This was not a game, and she was not small prey. Kirima ducked into a low crouch, sweeping my incoming leg, though she was too late. Or so I thought.

Something hooked my leg.

Both legs flew into the air and my eyes snapped wide open. She had used a qi ability, but she was far too young to have unlocked one. As I plummeted toward the ground, Kirima jabbed a half-curled fist to crush my throat. With no time to think, I reacted. I snatched her wrist and used her momentum to pirouette midair.

Her teeth gritted fiercely as she slammed into the ground, my elbow crashing into the center of her chest. I felt a pop as the air caught in her lungs and her chest collapsed on itself.

Immediately, I shot to my feet, yelling, "Master Kashvi!"

Kirima couldn't speak to be able to yield, but there was no denying the match was finished.

Master Kashvi was already rushing from the raised seats for the masters. The other masters watched in a mixture of awe and indignation. Kirima was the youngest heir, but a complete victory was nothing to ignore among those trained to subdue kingdoms. Master Feiyu stood, hands clutching the railing in front of him and feet rooted to the floor though his eyes burned to rush to his heir's side. He turned his burning gaze to me. His muscles were taut against his brown robes and his toes clenched the ground through his sandals.

"We will have words," I could hear his soul seethe.

A gasp filled my ears, bringing unexpected relief to something inside me as Master Kashvi withdrew a step. Compassion had been relinquished from my master. Why would I offer it to these charlatans?

Kirima took several heavy breaths as a tear slipped down her cheek. A suffocating heaviness clawed into my lungs as I watched her struggle to pull herself together. I tried emptily to remind myself I would restore the balance to all of the lineages. Her fall would only be temporary, unlike the Dragon's if I failed. But the beads of devastation in her eyes stung in my heart like the day Master Hito told me we were finished.

"I failed," she whispered to herself.

"You fought bravely," I said, bowing at the waist.

Kirima stood on shaky legs and returned the bow. Given the beating they gave me yesterday, even the other heirs were afraid they would lose in a fair fight. No one could truly blame her for the defeat. That was why Xael had been sent. I looked to the tunnel, but the boy was gone. I tensed, searching for him in the crowd and among the masters. Only masters sat on their stand, and too many people crowded the stands to find him in the masses.

"Victory to the Dragon heir," Master Kashvi announced.

The stands erupted in applause. Worry chipped my confidence. Where had Xael gone? I looked to the crowd again and recessed to the tunnel, forcing myself to walk at a calm pace. How had I lost him in the mere moments I was gone?

8

"Xael!" I yelled from the mouth of the tunnel where we had entered.

"Xael! Xael. Xael…" it echoed back.

My head whipped this way and that. How could he have disappeared so quickly? I trudged down the brick path. In such a short time, he couldn't be far. Anger burned in my veins as worry flooded my mind. Criminals would love to get their hands on a young, resilient boy. Why would he run off in the first place?

In my fear, I nearly tripped over my pack and its contents strewn on the ground around it. My heart dropped in my chest. I knelt, clutching it tightly. It was surrounded by scuff marks on the pristine path. I searched ahead, but there were no more marks. Someone snatched him, he struggled to drop the pack for me, and they carried him off.

I sprinted for the back entrance where they must have taken

him. It wasn't far. Just another few hundred feet and I could climb to the roofs for a vantage point. How was I supposed to find him among the hundreds of thousands of people?

A chilling torrent of air extinguished every torch in the hall.

"Run! It's—" Xael called out before someone muzzled his voice.

Where had that echo originated? I closed my eyes to listen. No good. I needed light.

"Breathe," Master Hito had constantly reminded. I took a deep breath in, filling every inch of my burning lungs until I felt they might burst. I turned around and expelled the burning air into a breath of fire, singeing the ground and alighting the wooden bases of the torches. Light flooded the tunnel, bringing my eyes to a handful of archers facing me, bowstrings pulled taut.

A hooded man towered over Xael with an arm around his neck, but he wasn't the only captive. Pochi's apprentice slumped, bound and discarded, on the ground.

The hooded figure chuckled. "New tricks, little Dragon, too bad you're pinned here. Kneel and we'll make it quick for both of you."

He stroked one knuckle down Xael's cheek. Xael drilled his wrathful eyes into mine, burning for action. I shook my head and glanced toward the torches, hoping the boy caught on.

"Hmph, the word of an assassin is as intangible as the wind," I replied.

"And yet the wind blows with the force of a thousand men when it is angry," he said, motioning for his archers to stand ready. Their clothes had clearly been made to blend into the night.

"Let my soldier go, and I will let you live this once," I bit out. Five archers were child's play, but he could slit Xael's throat before I got there.

"That's rich coming from a dying lineage," the man boldly antagonized.

With a mirthless laugh, I quipped, "The only thing dying today is a few thugs in a tunnel."

"That's enough baseless arrogance." The man shoved Xael at another assailant. Xael played along and stumbled into the archer who quickly grabbed the boy by his shoulders. I scoffed. Too easy.

The ringleader spread his arm arrogantly and clapped them together. A blast of wind extinguished the fire once again. I dove forward, rolling quietly beneath zinging arrows. No one could adjust to the shift in light that quickly. I grabbed the first archer's bow as he knocked another arrow. I slung it aside and reached for him, but the man vanished. I growled and jumped at where the large hooded man had been, but he too was gone. More arrows shot vaguely in my direction. They were regaining their vision. I heard another man cry out from where Xael had been. I collided with the boy, knocking him to the ground. With Xael beneath me, I was safe to exhale a cloud of smoke through my nostrils.

"Where'd he go?"

"He can't be far!"

I drew a breath and released fire at them, clashing with a wall of air. I leaned into the gust as it cleared the smoke. I exhaled another burst of fire to light my way, but they had all vanished. I clutched my chest, coughing against the painful scorching sensation in my airway.

Xael ran to the other boy and struggled against the ropes. I walked over and knelt beside them. They were both alive. I channeled qi into one finger to form a claw and cut at the ropes. Meanwhile, Xael flicked his fingers just beneath the apprentice's jawline.

"Dragon heir!" the boy shot to life, scraping the severed ropes from his wrists. "A woman with broken ribs and auburn eyes—Master Pochi said to slip out and come to you, but I got—"

I was already out of the tunnel before he could finish. If these men were in league with that woman, I had to get there before they warned her I was alive. With any luck, I would get there in time to finish what I started.

The streets surrounding the coliseum were cluttered with people. Some passed their money around, bets lost or won, while beggar children snatched coin pouches from others.

I waded through the masses until I reached the freedom of the alleyways. I looked to the sky and took a deep, savory breath that soured in an instant. Smoke smothered the moon and my breath. It was coming from Pochi's clinic.

Xael kept up surprisingly well, but I lost the other boy during one of the zigzags. As I got closer, shouts reached my ears. Armored guards barked orders to smother the flames before they spread.

How had the assassins learned of Pochi's involvement? And why had the lesser assassin come after me? In my heart, I knew this was my fault. I shouldn't have mentioned any of this to Pochi. I should have left him out of it completely. I should have done exactly as my master said. Why was I so bad at listening to him?

As I burst back onto the main street, smoke bombarded my senses. Flames engulfed the clinic in a horrifying blaze, billowing stacks of smoke that clouded what was once a canopy of stars.

A line of men threw buckets of well water on the raging fire as it whipped into the sky. Before I knew what I was doing, I barreled into the house. Flames licked at my skin, immediately reminding me to hurl the pack to Xael outside and wrap cloth around my face. The heat was bearable, but it singed my un-guarded hair.

"Pochi!" I roared above the breaking beams, disintegrating in the heat of the blaze.

A distant cry reached my ears followed by splashing. I ran through the opening that was once guarded by a draping carpet. Now it was only ashes met my feet. Even the clothes on my body couldn't block the searing heat.

"Pochi!" I called, seeing a broken body in the smoking sauna. I jumped into the pool in the center of the room and scooped him into my arms.

He coughed weakly. "San?"

"I'll get you out!" I said, looking for the nearest exit.

The entrance crumbled in a puff of smoke and burning wood.

The ceiling shuddered as if reacting to my fear. If it fell, would the impact kill me or would I drown?

"San," he struggled with cracked lips. "Too late."

He coughed blood, taking a hand off his neck. Red spurted like an open spring. I snapped his hand back in place.

"She went…" he wheezed, pointing to the rear. "Wanted you to burn…"

"Pochi, I need you," I cried, dipping us both in the water again. There had to be another way. I had to find a way out. "You're all I have left of him!"

Pochi's sagging skin pulled tight around his burns. Even if I knew a way out, he wasn't going to make it. His splitting lips tinted purple even in the blazing room. Another beam crashed to my right, billowing smoke at us.

Time had won. *She* had won. We were trapped and Pochi had lost too much blood.

"Her arm…"

Pochi's head rolled limply to the side.

I shook him desperately. "What about it? It was limp? I know, Pochi, what about it?" My heart raced faster than a horse and tears evaporated off my cheeks.

I pulled him close, trying to guard him against the burning air. Somehow, he felt cold. I cried out in anguish and rage. Ashes rained from the ceiling and the walls bulged. I had to run, but there was nowhere to go. Flames encroached. Ashes rained. Smoke choked my lungs and bleared my eyes.

Beyond the smoke, the back wall crumbled as a hazy Xael

burst through it, wooden plank in hand. He stood covering his face with an arm. I flew out into the cool air. The clinic crashed behind me, a mere pile of timber and ash.

"Master Pochi…" The apprentice had finally caught up.

"I'm sorry," I said, setting Pochi on the open street. I swallowed, seeing the shriveled man, soaked in an ugly mixture of bloody water and covered in blistering burns, many of which were so severe they had already popped. I unwound the scorched cloth from my face and wrapped it around his neck. Not so much as a wheeze left his lungs. There was nothing I could do…again.

The air was frosty in my smoke-filled lungs. Every breath felt like a bag of needles stabbing the inside of my chest. I doubled over myself, coughing uncontrollably.

"Are you hurt?" Xael asked, putting a hand on my shoulder, and immediately recoiling. He winced and shook it as if he had grabbed a burning ember.

I spewed a breath of soot and replied, "I'll be fine. That witch, however—"

I abruptly fell into a coughing fit, clearing the last of the debris from my airway. I had no healer, no support, only an impossible goal and endless barricades. Worst of all, I knew I had disappointed Master Hito.

Pochi was more than a healer to him. Master Hito had trained under him. He was a friend truer than I was an heir, and I let them kill him.

No. I might as well have killed him, walking into his clinic in broad daylight.

In feigned stoicism, Pochi's apprentice snuffled and said, "I need to bury him. His family is all gone."

"We will help," I said.

I carried Pochi's body past a chain of civilians carrying buckets of water from the nearest well to the diminishing rubble. Eyes tracked us into Pochi's family plot. What would the rumors say? Would they grow and spread until the Dragon heir was not just forsaken, but a murderer?

"I'm so sorry," I breathed over his dead body.

He couldn't hear me, but I needed to tell him I never meant to drag him into this. I never meant to get anyone killed. Death in war was one thing, but to bury a friend in the homeland felt wrong. Pochi was the only person in this godforsaken city who stood by my master's name. My presence was his damnation.

None of this was supposed to happen. Why did my world keep crumbling around me? Why could I never do enough to stop it?

Tears spoke the words I wasn't strong enough to say as I rested Pochi in the casket he had carved from a sandalwood tree. Even as long as I had lived among the Xinyuan people, it seemed a morbid tradition to prepare your own grave. Still, as with everything he did, it was a work of art. Intricate carvings of dragons and waves covered every inch of the yellow, fragrant casket.

Having none of my own, I recited his and Master Hito's words just as they used to echo to each other.

"Life is so short and yet so beautiful."

Pochi's apprentice choked back sobs.

"May they find each other on the other side."

"What happened to you?" Kirima met us on the street in front of our lodging.

"Aren't you still upset with me?" I evaded the question. Xael followed silently with his head bowed. His sunken shoulders told of an exhaustion deeper than the ocean.

"I never was." She turned her head away. "I have much to learn before I can stand against you."

I raised a single, unconvinced eyebrow. She was trying, but bitterness escaped her frigid eyes. This wasn't the competition anyone wanted. She could blame me all she liked. Really, she was right to do so. It was my persistence, after all, that caused all of this—her disgrace and Pochi's death.

I had lost my integrity wrapping Pochi up in all of this. My master specifically told me not to involve anyone else. He told me to let it all go, but I couldn't. I couldn't let anything go. Not the emperor's unreasonable edict nor his unjust abandonment of our lineage. Neither the lineages debasing my master nor their scheming egos.

Kirima's gaze lingered on my charred uniform. "I heard a building burned…"

"Assassins," I grunted as I trudged up the pagoda stairs.

"Assassins?" she whispered coming alongside. "Come for you?"

"Initially," I said, turning a distrustful side-eye to her. "Someone has lost all virtue. Pochi was killed."

Her jaw slacked, speechless. Mistrust escaped my squinted eyes as I struggled to believe her shock. She had the most to gain from my disappearance.

"You can't possibly think *I* am responsible for the assassins?" She gasped.

"Why not?" I snapped, removing the space between us. I glared down at her small frame.

Kirima clicked her teeth and wrinkled her nose at me. "It would be a little late to kill you, don't you think?"

I stopped at that. It made alarmingly more sense than my suspicion.

"If you think it's one of us, why not join tonight?"

I considered that for a longing moment. Tradition had the heirs spend the first night raising a toast to those who had paved the way. It was a show of gratitude to the lineages and masters who set a bar that we could only surpass, because of the work they did to steer us from their mistakes.

"I am not welcome among the heirs," I said, shutting it down. It would only stir up trouble for myself and the others.

"If I am welcome, they must also accept you, as per the emperor's edict," Kirima said. She forced a smile that didn't reach her ears.

"Hm," I sighed. "As fun as it sounds to have drinks with people who hate me, I can't leave Xael."

"I'll be fine," Xael spoke for the first time in hours. His eyes fell uncharacteristically to the side. I had only known the boy for a day, but this brooding contrasted with the Xael I had come to know. "You don't have to babysit me."

"I never said I was babysitting you. You had to earn your place here."

A smile stole onto his face. "Then you know I'll be fine."

Kirima agreed, "Master Feiyu says the boy is formidable—why not bring him?"

I glanced between them. I thought the Leopard was just goading me before the duels, but now I wondered. How had Xael come so quickly? How had he healed so quickly?

I hummed with a warning. "Sure. We will join. But tell the others they will be wise to keep their hands off me tonight."

I turned into my room to change. As Xael slid the door shut, I directed my qi at him. I didn't intend to hurt him, but I wanted him to fear I would.

Xael spun with a sharp inhale. His pupils dilated and he faltered. His back pressed into the door. His palms flattened against the bamboo as his shoulders climbed to his ears.

"You're not just a foot soldier," I accused. "I can't figure how you made it down the Eastern Cliffs, nor how you kept up with me tonight. You were sound asleep but somehow knew where I had gone earlier. Even Master Feiyu sees something different about you." I laid out my pieces of evidence one by one. Sweat built on the boy's brow with every item. He flinched as I stepped toward him. "Who *are* you?"

"I am Xael Binturong," he uttered.

"Binturong… A lineage?" I pressed.

"It…once was," Xael said. "Now it's just me."

"Hm," I mused. "That still does not explain your abilities. You're too young to have been trained extensively."

Xael shifted uncomfortably. He dragged a toe on the ground as if he was betraying a great secret.

"Explain yourself, Xael."

"You call the source of your power *qi*, right?"

I nodded.

"When you inherit a lineage, even one as small as the Binturong, it comes with certain…*qi* abilities. 'Inheritors', or 'masters' as you call them, can see when that has unlocked in someone else."

I postulated, "So, Master Feiyu saw that in you?"

He nodded.

"And me?"

Xael bit his lip, choosing his words. "I don't know. Your *qi* is overwhelming, but it's different. It's like Master Hito unlocked your potential before, um, before he was supposed to."

It made sense, but I wasn't sold on the story. "If you have a… sixth sense, how did you get blindsided by the assassins?"

"It was like they just appeared. Like the Leopard, except I can feel I'm being stalked by him. It seemed like the archers didn't exist until they, well, did," he said. "I would have fought back, I promise, but they said they would kill you while you weren't watching if I tried to warn you." He cringed, putting a hand to his head.

It would be too showy to act in front of thousands, even from a distance. The assassins would garner the fury of all the lineages by striking in the middle of something sacred. They would have to be truly desperate to do something that reckless. Tonight was a statement. *We can take everything.* Only, they had no idea I already lost what mattered most to me—Master Hito. Which begged the question, why did I not have these inheritor abilities Xael spoke of.

"And why don't I have that sixth sense?" I challenged.

"I—"

Three knocks thrummed on the door. I pulled Xael behind me. We would finish this discussion later. I coiled my fist and threw the door open. Baihu stood with a cocksure grin and folded arms that were as scarred as his master.

"Our fight is not for another four days," he said with his nose to the ceiling. "But if you wish…"

"That would violate the rules," I said.

"Like master, like student."

I forced my fist open before I killed the arrogant prick. "Why are you here?"

He smiled with pure white teeth. "Kirima said you were going to join, so we were waiting to toast."

I snagged a clean robe from a hanger. "How sweet."

Xael and I followed the Tiger heir up the pagoda's overhanging roofs. On the very top, the other five heirs dangled their legs over the edge facing the palace. I glanced from Jai, a head above the rest even seated, to Baihu. Neither looked to be scheming and neither would have been able to keep it off their face. I took a deep breath and joined the line of dangling feet.

From all the way up here, you could see the torches and hanging lanterns lighting the maze of greenery that surrounded the Marble Palace. The pristine white swirls of its walls glistened even at this distance. Under a blanket of stars, we shared a toast.

"To those who came before—may we honor them by furthering their arts," Zimo toasted softly, as the longest-standing heir.

"May we honor them," we reprised and took a swig of drink.

"I heard you had an exciting night," Shintaro hissed in my ear. I shoved space between us.

"Yeah," Jai joined. "Kirima says you jumped into a burning building?"

I sent Kirima a betrayed glare.

"That explains the filthy uniform," Baihu muttered.

"I heard you carried someone out," Zimo said.

"He was already dead," I said, crossing my arms. Zimo's gaze dropped with pursed lips.

Mehnaz bobbed her shaved head forward meeting my gaze past the line of heirs. "How'd you survive that?"

"There was a pool of water," I said. "And Xael here busted a wall to break me out."

I wanted to be sure only the traitor knew I had *qi* abilities

"Whoa," she swung to Xael and poked his arms.

"It was gonna fall anyway," Xael said, fiddling with his thumbs and kicking his feet beneath the overhang.

"It'sss an odd time of the year for a fire," Shintaro said.

"Anytime is odd for arson," I replied, making sure to watch the others. Zimo and Mehnaz's eyes widened, but the others either expected as much or hid it well.

"Arssson?" Shintaro asked, "You're sss-certain?"

Exasperated, I stood and said, "The only hearth in that clinic is beneath the water. How do you suppose fire spread from there?" Xael arose to my side.

"Give it a rest," Kirima said. "He's had a long enough night."

"Sit back down, San." Baihu patted the glazed tiling and changed the subject. "Do you think we'll be sent after the north-western kingdom of ice soon?"

"Not a chance," I said, my words taking on a sharper edge than intended.

"Why not?" the Tiger heir asked.

I debated before returning to my seat. Zimo was right, exhaustion and desperation were clouding my decisions. This was the one night that the heirs, no matter what age, sat together, teasing and rumoring. Beneath all the responsibility of keeping the emperor's noble appearance, these were the only friends I had. I thought that would mean more to them and to Master Hito's comrades. He tried to warn me otherwise.

With all eyes on me, I took a breath and rationalized, "We

would need to start an assault like that at the first breath of spring. Not to mention the resources our soldiers would require to survive."

"The emperor sent scouts," Jai joined with a conspiratorial grin. I tried to pull the annoyance from my growing scowl. I wanted nothing more than to smack that grin right off his face. There was nothing fun about sending soldiers to that death trap.

"And they never returned from the icy wasteland. There is no fruit in taking that land," Kirima said. "It would be better to continue west to the Volgrians."

"But then they could cut our supplies if they wished," Baihu pointed out.

"Who are 'they'?" I challenged, "When the Dragon and Rhino neared the wasteland that borders our kingdoms, we saw nothing but snow and hazardous terrain. Who knows if it's even inhabited."

"An easy victory, then," Shintaro said, sipping the translucent wine. His eyes held a smirk as he glanced at me from the side. I hated how he always knew when something agitated me. It was like he reveled in crawling under my skin, for the sheer enjoyment of my irritation.

"A worthless victory," Baihu countered.

"We would be better expanding over the Volgrians," I agreed.

"Say, San," Baihu asked, "when did you learn that reversal you did on Kirima? I've never seen that before."

"Master Hito taught me last week," I said, stretching my arms above my head.

"Last week?" Jai shouted, earning a shush from half the heirs. "And you banked your victory on it?"

I smiled fondly at the memory. "I didn't expect Kirima to land the sweep. But once she did, I figured she'd be coming for the jugular."

"Hey, 'Have due caution in defense, and sure victory in the swift attack,'" she defended, quoting the first Leopard master.

"Hm, and 'Allow the enemy to provide his own defeat.' Or rather, 'her own defeat' in this instance," I quoted back with a wink. Master Hito was always reading his books aloud while I tried to meditate.

"Bold words for you," Jai stated, sloshing rice wine over the rim of his glass.

"Bolder even for you to speak, considering your loss tonight," Baihu taunted back, clinking his glass to Jai's.

Jai's growl was interrupted by Zimo's soft question. "What will you request of the emperor if you do succeed?"

"The Dragon master will make his request," I corrected.

"What do you suppose Master Hito will request?" he asked again, tapping a finger on the tiled roof and glancing at the others, whose eyes all rested on me. "I think we would all like things to return to the way they were."

Things would never return to the way they were. All of the faith and trust I was taught to have in the lineages and the emperor had long since evaporated. I would never trust them again.

"I presume a means of repayment that does not involve our soldiers." I couldn't lie to Zimo, but it seemed unwise to tell the whole truth.

"I think your sssignet bearer is going to topple over." Shintaro poked a startled response out of Xael, who was more asleep than awake.

I helped him to his feet and bid the others farewell. "Until tomorrow. I look forward to our duels."

"Hey, Dragon," Baihu called. I looked over my shoulder at the Tiger heir. "This was a respect for tradition. After tonight, you and your prey don't have a place among us."

I would have rolled my eyes and let it go if Kirima's whole demeanor hadn't melted.

"Tiger, I wonder…" I said, slowly spinning on my heels. "How much confidence must the emperor lack in you to only let me fight you after he intends for me to be greatly injured?"

Indignation consumed Baihu as he stood to challenge with knuckles as white as the moon. Jai jumped to his feet, faster than I had ever seen him move. He grabbed Baihu's vibrating shoulder as the others watched with roused expressions.

"Don't stoop to his disgrace," Jai said.

The smile twitching on my face vanished with the sound of a disembodied voice. "San. A word."

"Of course, Master Feiyu." I dipped my head and dropped from roof to roof until I reached the bottom, where the Leopard showed himself. "Do you ever get tired of that?"

"It takes more effort to show myself," he said, folding his arms.

With a deep, full breath, the master flickered out of sight and materialized back at the end of his exhale. For the first time, I noticed how shallow his breaths were. Anyone with any kind of formal training knew to take deep breaths to maximize harnessing *qi* and steadying the mind. If his insinuation was true that he had to breathe shallow to be seen…why show me, the bane and embarrassment of the empire?

"You mean, you could stay invisible all the time?" Xael asked with the drowsiest starry eyes.

"San could too, if he had been of a different lineage."

"If I recall the story, you told Master Hito it was unwise to take a non-noble as an heir," I aired, unsure what the point of this conversation was.

His voice hushed.

"And yet a fine heir you made," he said. "And I am truly pleased that he passed over a noble child of his own homeland to have you. I am most pleased to call Kirima my heir, just as he was proud to call you his…but you have much to be desired as a master."

"Baihu was insulting your heir—"

"My heir that you brutalized tonight," he scolded.

"Brutalized?" I snapped. "Kirima is far too stubborn to yield with your lineage's status on the line. I ended it as kindly as I could."

I left off that the emperor was really the one to be blamed for Kirima's suffering.

He smothered a look of pride before he said, "Even so, only the Tiger sees any slight against the Leopard lineage for losing."

"I wish they had been so sensible with my master," I rumbled.

Master Feiyu shook his head. "We never despised Master Hito in our hearts. The emperor spoke and we adhered. His words are law…"

I puffed smoke. If the emperor wanted his words to be law, he ought to be the one enforcing them. "Did you just come to scold me for Baihu's lack of regulation?"

"I came to keep you out of trouble," he claimed.

"Oh, how considerate of you," I replied thanklessly with a mocking, showman's bow.

"Sanav, you cannot reinstate the legacy alone—"

I shot back, "And where was that consideration when Master Hito needed it?"

"Fine!" he barked. Xael flinched behind me but I was too angry to notice the beast I provoked. "I was wrong. I should have sent an eagle, or better yet come myself. But I didn't and the only thing I can think to do is help his stubborn, bull-headed heir."

I blinked, trying to comprehend what I was hearing. Masters did not apologize to each other, and certainly not to an heir. It was a matter of poise. I opened my mouth but nothing came out. I blinked away the shock. If he really was sorry, that was all the more reason I couldn't involve him in this. I already killed one of Master Hito's friends—I couldn't stand to do it again.

"Master, are you ok?" Kirima dropped from the roof, not a sound to indicate her landing.

"When you grow up, come talk to me," Master Feiyu growled at me and then disappeared again.

I waved off Kirima's bewildered expression. "I should rest."

I must have woken a hundred times that night. It was like reliving a bizarre version of my life as an heir. I saw things happen in a way they hadn't, and fought foes possessed by demons I never saw. Yet I didn't expect the terrors that awaited each time I awoke and fell back into sleep. I peeled my blanket from my sweat-soaked body and opened the window to watch the dark blue lose its grip on the horizon.

"Master San," Xael muttered groggily, "Is everything ok?"

"Hm?" I absentmindedly asked, recalling the last dream of a fight with a burning eagle. The flames burned Pochi's decrepit eyes as the eagle had slid its talons through his throat. *That's not what happened!*

"You look lost," an indistinct voice said.

"What?" I found Xael kneeling behind me. "Were you talking to me?"

"I asked if everything's ok," he said with gently lifted eyebrows. He rubbed the deep circles under his eyes.

"Yes. What makes you say I look lost?" I asked, clearing my own eyes of sleep.

"I didn't say that," he hastened to reply. "Lost in thought, maybe."

"Ah. Well, shall we get breakfast, see if our uniforms are mended, and show our faces at a few dueling sites?" Our forces were robust enough with the lack of war to dwindle their numbers, but it was my responsibility to spur the hearts of the people by watching duels.

Xael's eyes lit, whether for food or fighting, I could not tell. When my eyes tired of watching laymen spar, Xael and I headed to Pochi's burial site. We stopped at a store of relics to purchase a dragon statue to guard his grave. He was proud to serve my lineage and I was proud to claim him. I owed this man who had healed countless of my injuries far more, and yet it was all I could do now.

The store was cluttered in organized chaos. An approximate section break between each kind of animal was all that separated the items. Gold, bronze, and jade could be found side by side, so long as both relics were roughly dragon-esque. The jade seemed especially appropriate for Pochi, a man with the noblest soul.

The longer I browsed, the less I wanted to remain in the shop. My head spun as the statues all seemed to converge on me. Where was Xael?

Xael reached for a burning bird necklace dangling from a

stone Vermillion statue. "Don't touch that!" I smacked Xael's hand. Who even followed that dead lineage anymore?

"I'm sorry for your loss," the shopkeeper said.

"What?" I said, snapping around to face the man with a magnifying circle over his right eye. With so many trinkets vying for my attention, I had missed the scrawny man behind his counter.

"The jade dragon caught your eye. It calls to the grieved." His creaking voice and piercing eyes gave him the charisma of a pirate. Judging by the oddities surrounding me, it might have been an accurate assessment of the man.

"How much for it?" I asked.

"Twen'y coins," he said. "A worthy gift for those who have gone before, no?"

"Those who have gone before"…that was the saying of the heirs.

"You recognize me?" I asked, sizing him from head to toe. He was lanky, hardly any muscle on his frame. One scarred hand rested on the wooden counter while the other waved with his speech.

"I recognize that signet on the boy, and only one Dragon would have the gall to waltz aroun' town with it beside 'im," he said. The bright red circlet on his face was meant to stand out. It did its job a little too well.

"Hm, I suppose," I reasoned. "Ten coins for the dragon. That is what it's worth."

"I might agree if I were selling to a commoner or noble, but to do business with the Dragon may cost me. Sixteen."

I grumbled. Haggling was the last thing I cared to do for Pochi's guardian stone and this man knew it. "Thirteen gold and we call it a deal."

"Fifteen."

"Fine," I tossed a bag of fifteen imperial coins at him. "Let's go, Xael."

"Nice doing business," the shopkeeper hollered as the door slapped shut, the bell resounding as it did.

I rested the dragon atop the crisp, white headstone. "Pochi: The Great Healer" was carved into the stone today. Xael stood silently at my side as the minutes ticked by. Why had I dragged him into this mess? Master Hito told me to leave everyone out of this. "Worthless," he had ridiculed my striving. "Dangerous," he called my efforts. As always, my master was right…I should have listened.

A chirping sparrow flew past me onto the large wooden arch that marked the end of the garden and the beginning of the meager home. I walked along the path that split Pochi's front yard into two neatly tended gardens of herbs and spices. The irrigation nursed each plant like a newborn child. His house stood as a dwarf at the end of the path. A straw roof frayed at the edges, flaxen needles coating the ground surrounding the home's simple four walls. I knocked on the weathered door, an apology prepared for a family I had never met.

I remembered his apprentice's words when no one came. The boy was all he had. I slid the door to the side and entered the dark house. The only thing notable about the interior was its lack of furniture. Unwelcoming floorboards creaked and groaned as if telling me they had finished their work. With only three rooms to call his own, it was clear his clinic was his true home.

"There's something in here," Xael called from another room.

"Hm?" I rounded the corner. Xael pointed at a red, leather-bound tome resting atop the only table in the room. I passed a stack of empty vials matching those he kept in the clinic and opened a window to bring light and fresh air into the stuffy study room. The book rested next to a cracked inkwell that had long since dried up. I blew a layer of dust off the top revealing a beautiful cover. A yellow dragon had been embossed on the cover along with the title *The Yellow Dragon*.

"It is part of our lineage. A person with the title of Yellow Dragon embodies wisdom, strength, and the hope of a fruitful harvest."

Xael blinked at me. "How is a person supposed to embody harvest?"

"Um…" It was a fair question, but one I had no idea how to answer. "Let's see if this book explains."

I carefully turned to the beginning of the book. The pages were thick and coated with something slick and clear. Someone had taken great care to ensure the knowledge within would never fade.

"What does it say?" Xael asked, dragging his toe in a circle on the floor. His hands rubbed the seams of his pants.

I started at a point on the page, when it struck me. Of course, Xael had not been taught to read… How could our soldiers teach what they did not know? Reading was a simple means to separate nobles from commoners. I would have to teach him, but not today.

"It says," I paused and cleared my throat. "'To my faithful first captain—May your retirement bring you fulfillment and peace. Never forget the Dragon teachings, Pochi the Yellow. Write them down, that our dynasty may continue forever. To the fortunate Red Dragon, may this text bring peace and temperance. To the White, discernment and caution. To the Azure, depth and insight. To the Yellow, humility and hope. To the Black, alarm and conviction.'"

I never knew Pochi was a captain in the Dragon lineage and a first captain at that. He never mentioned it, nor did Master Hito. I wondered if his blindness had caused his retirement.

"Which Dragon are you?" Xael asked.

"Hm, I don't know," I said. "That is usually assigned at the end of one's life."

"Well, what are the options? I bet I can guess." He smiled as if presented with a challenge.

"Sit down," I said. "The first lesson talks about the Dragons."

Xael sat on his knees, bright eyes beaming like a child ready for a bedtime tale. I cleared my throat and began again as the handwriting shifted.

"'A lineage as old and diverse as mankind. With this knowledge comes great power, and thus the duty to choose its descendants carefully, lest a Black Dragon be unleashed on the world. A Red Dragon will bring good fortune and gladness; White brings justice and virtue; Azure offers peace and revival; Yellow gives wisdom and understanding; Gold provides prosperity and true power. But the Black Dragon bestows vengeance and, with it, the

corrupt power of death. All be warned, lest they fall into the way of the Black Dragon, which breeds mourning and demands the shedding of innocent blood." I swallowed at the changing tone.

Xael piped up, "Obviously you're the Gold Dragon. That's the one that talked about power, right?"

I laughed. "There has not been a Golden Dragon since…" I scoured my memories, "…I don't know when."

There was something about a Golden Dragon, but it danced just beyond my reach. "Master Hito talked about a Golden Dragon once, but I think it was in a fable."

"I guess you can be the first," Xael said.

I rolled my eyes but a smile snuck onto my face. I closed the book and slipped it into my pack. "Let's go before we're late."

On our way back to the pagoda, we passed the rubble that was Pochi's clinic and snagged our pressed uniforms from the adjacent cleaner. Anger climbed up my throat as I itched for a rematch with the assassins. I'd had a chance and I squandered it.

In no time, the moon was high and I stood at the edge of the tunnel, watching Kirima and Baihu take their places in the arena. As unfair as it seemed to have her face me and Baihu first, none of the heirs were an easy fight and we took particularly little pleasure in degrading our rivals.

Still, I cringed watching Baihu completely dominate the positioning. Kirima tried to sweep, but he gave her more credit than I and bobbed his leg behind. He hooked it around her planted leg and yanked the footing from right under her. Baihu crashed into her, landing an open-grip strike to her windpipe. I scratched at my sympathetically achy throat.

Shintaro and Jai sparred on an even skill level. Neither was especially equipped for the other since Jai's strategy was to break defenses and Shintaro's was to target weak spots. It made for a longer, back-and-forth battle where the first big mistake lost the match. That went to Jai—he fell for a clever bait, bulldozing Shintaro, who slipped around like a constrictor, cinching his legs around Jai's thick neck. He ducked and bobbed out of reach until Jai succumbed to the loss of oxygen.

"Now entering: Mehnaz of the Monkey and Sanav of the Dragon!" Master Kashvi announced.

Mehnaz crouched with both fists on the ground, draped in her thick forest-green uniform. A deep-brown sash wrapped around her uniform instead of a belt. It showed her experience and doubled as a deadly weapon, but one she was not permitted to use in this duel. What would the emperor ask of her lineage when she failed to stop me? What was I inflicting upon her soldiers?

As soon as the gong rang, we charged toward each other. She barreled into my waist with her hands tossed over her head as both a cover and preparation to slam. She deflected my first strike, and I dodged her fists. She slammed both hands at my feet. As I jumped back, she grabbed my ankles and ripped them into the air. I could feel Master Hito's outrage as I plummeted to Mehnaz's area of expertise.

As soon as my back hit the ground, I rebounded with my hands. Mehnaz took a knee to the gut on her way to saddle me. She slammed her hands into my shoulders to drive herself above my knees and onto my chest. My back cracked against the stonework. I cringed and jabbed a pathetic punch into her gut. From my back, I didn't have the power to pierce her ribs.

I cursed my compassion for dulling my senses. My soldiers needed me. The emperor had all but declared war on me and *my* lineage. Simply winning this fight wasn't enough—I needed to win without injury, or else Baihu would easily exploit my weakness.

I curled just in time to dodge her slamming fist. I thrusted my hips, vaulting Mehnaz nearly into a face-plant. I twisted violently, spinning myself on top. Her legs squeezed around my waist, fighting for control. I waylaid into her center.

Mehnaz was too busy blocking to counter until the last second, when I launched a kill strike at her floating rib. She kicked my knee out to steal my power, but not enough. I felt the rib pop and sink into her center mass. She kicked me off her pinned leg and rolled away from me.

Mehnaz clutched her side and wobbled to her feet. Had this been a normal year, she would yield, but too much rode on these fights. She risked her life in continuing to fight with a dislodged rib. I had a sure victory, Mehnaz just refused to admit it. And they said I lacked nobility as one of the conquered.

I swooped a kick at the edge of my range. She escaped beneath, hands landing on the ground to support her as she shot a leg around mine and toppled me to the ground. She climbed onto my chest and hammered a fist at my face.

"Not once but twice in one match?" I heard my master chastise.

I bobbed my head to the right and let her fist scrape against the stone. She would be ready for the launch this time. As the other fist fell, I curled up and shot my hand to the right, brushing the inside of her arm. I covered my head with my left arm and snapped the side of my right fist into the side of her neck. She limply fell over me like a blanket.

"Match," Master Kabir announced for the crowd's sake. "Dragon lineage."

I carefully rolled Mehnaz to the side, cradling her ribs and head. Master Kashvi could work her magic.

As I approached Xael behind the masters, I received several half-hearted congratulations. The Tiger master looked down at me over the bridge of his nose.

"You have improved immensely since the last festival," Master Kabir noted.

"With the lull in war, Master Hito had more time to train me," I said.

"I look forward to your duel with Baihu—he has also improved."

We'll see how much, I thought to myself. The night was as bright as the day under the nearly complete moon. Somehow it seemed brighter in the capital than anywhere else, as if it concentrated its blessing here. Still, I preferred the open air of our mountain fortress, where the wind whipped like a sailing ship and the sun shone in equal majesty.

I took to the back alleys, where shadows stilled the light and quiet hedged the noisy streets. I watched the sky, stars drowned out by the moonlight. An occasional cloud passed over the moon, casting the torchless passages into complete darkness. In those moments, I listened, suspended in nothingness.

"Can you tell me about Master Hito?" Xael broke the silence.

"Didn't you meet him?" I asked with a raised eyebrow. He could often be found among the soldiers, offering lessons and encouraging them.

"I'm a pretty new addition," Xael said, "By the time I came, he only ever spent time training you. Everyone thought a big war was coming until…well…" He swallowed hard.

"He saw us as a family," I said.

"You *are* his heir," Xael pointed out the obvious.

"No, I mean him, me, Captain Chiyo, the other captains, and all the rest of the soldiers," I explained. "He said when the battles came, all that mattered was the responsibility each person had for the other's lives. That is how a battle is won—by carrying the weight of the soldier's life to your right and to your left, like a brother or sister."

"You really think that way?" he asked skeptically.

"Hm, well, it's different for me," I said. "I carry the weight of every soldier, like a father for his sons. Master Hito taught that if I lacked strategy, self-control, humility, or confidence, it would not be I who suffered most, but each of you, and that would be unforgivable."

Xael scrunched his face as if it were a foreign concept. "Are the other lineages like that?"

"Some are similar, but no—Master Hito saw leadership as servitude. I don't know of anyone else who sees it in such a backwards light. But there's something far more noble about it, don't you think?"

He nodded, but his lips pursed. "I guess so."

"But…?"

"But what's the point of working so hard to get it?" he asked.

I smiled. "Few are able to bear the responsibility of leadership; some cannot bear to watch lesser men abuse it."

"Well, what do you get out of it?" Xael had stopped walking, so I paused in the street.

"Hm, I get to watch my soldiers thrive," I responded earnestly, though my heart was heavy. I did want them to thrive, but I craved justice for my master more. He would say I was wrong for that, but how could I be? "And hopefully repay Master Hito for giving me a good name."

"You weren't a noble like Master Hito?"

I chuckled. "Oh no, I was as far from it as you get."

"A slave?"

"And one with a heap of debts from breaking into dojos."

Xael's eyes sparkled in the moonlight. That must have been how I looked on the pagoda steps that first night after Master Hito spared my life. I was thrown into the pagoda against my will, but I was a criminal nonetheless.

He asked, "Is that how you met him?"

"Not exactly. A few urchins thought it would be funny to throw me into the pagoda." A smile tugged at my ears, remembering what surely should have been my end.

"And then what?" He leaned closer.

"Before I could look for a way out, Master Hito found me. I thought I was a goner! He questioned me and I guess my answers satisfied him because the next thing I knew, he was teaching me a movement in the Dragon series, giving me a signet, and sending me on my way, just like that. I trained for two years, trying to figure the motions out on my own, while the Festival of Heirs approached."

"Did you?" He was totally lost in the story.

I brushed my fingers through my hair, reliving the memory. "Not like him…but the worst part was when Guo stole my signet."

He gasped, "Did you get it back?!"

"No, I never did, and I stayed a slave. The end."

He screwed up his whole face. I laughed and smacked him on the back, saying, "I actually didn't get the signet back, but I convinced my lord to enter me against Guo. Master Hito came to watch the signet bearer fight, but I used the kata he taught me to win."

"Wow…"

He skipped a step to catch up to me, readjusting the pack on his shoulders. I would never forget my master's kindness to me. Before he touched my life, I was nothing to anyone. If I had died, I would have been forgotten forever, just like my parents. He gave me a purpose and poise. Even if I couldn't convince the emperor to restore Master Hito's name among the masses, his subordinates would never forget his glory.

I tossed throughout the night, fighting off outlandish dreams. Master Hito knelt before me in a strange amalgamation of dragon and human aspects. His eyes were human, but his head was that of a dragon, with sharp teeth and flaring nostrils. His body held the shape of a human except for the long, jagged claws that replaced his fingers. Somehow, I was aware of my own misty form, and yet had no control of it.

In a flash, Master Hito raked his claws through his abdomen, roaring in agony. He gashed himself again and again while I struggled against invisible restraints. The dragon cried out to the moon for relief. *I failed him.* I was supposed to end his suffering. I thrashed free of my constraints carrying the momentum of my struggle into my swing. I descended on him as fire overtook the sky.

In a frozen moment, he looked up to me and said, "I made

a mistake." Time resumed and my momentum forced the punch through his neck.

"No!" I cried, sitting up in a pool of sweat.

"What's wrong?!" Xael scrambled for his knife.

I clenched my eyes shut and panted, "Nothing."

He scanned head to toe. After a suspicious gaze, he sheathed his knife. I rose and opened the window. Xael's growling stomach pulled my attention from the skyline.

"Sorry," he apologized with a hand over his stomach.

"Here," I set a few coins in his hand. "Bring steamed beef buns back."

"But the others—"

"Will do nothing. Their honor demands they win in the arena now," I said.

Xael huffed. "And those that already lost?"

"They have nothing to gain from my injury."

"But what—"

I interrupted by pointing to the door. He scrutinized as long as he dared and exited. It was not long before Shintaro leaned his shoulder against the doorframe. I folded my hands over my chest.

"To what do I owe this pleasure, Shintaro?"

"The pleasure is mine," he gave in a smarmy reply. "I'm just impresssed with your display."

"Get to the point."

"Curiosssity," he said, "I want to know what you expect to accomplish."

He shifted closer.

"We've already had this conversation," I grunted.

"But an audience with the emperor can't be your end goal." He smiled and whispered in my ear, "He would ask for what your master denied and we both know the Dragon never wavers."

I could feel the damp heat in my ear. I set my jaw and clipped, "I wish for the emperor to reconsider."

He chuckled and circled me. "Never lie to a liar, Sssan, it gives more information than the truth."

"Get out."

"Or what?"

"Or our match will not be short."

A twisted smile curved Shintaro's razor-thin lips. "How fierce. Are you afraid I'll find out about your precious plan? I already know…"

"Then why would you be here?" I forced a flat affect over the panic. It was a bluff. "And how could you possibly know?"

"Because Ssan, only one thing has ever changed the emperor's mind," he hissed, "*Assscension*." He slipped away with smugness dripping off him. "Sssee you at the parade…"

I watched him leave, unblinking. If he knew I intended to ascend…he couldn't know. He had to assume I would declare it for Master Hito. I suppressed a huff at the thought of putting my master in such a situation. Either way, I had to hope Shintaro would keep it to himself. If the masters knew, they would have their heirs out for my neck for blasphemy. I breathed heavily. He wouldn't have come if he intended to tell the others. He wanted something. What that was, I could not figure.

"They were out of steamed beef buns, so I got dumplings—I hope that's ok," Xael said reentering.

"That's great, Xael," I mindlessly replied, still churning over what Shintaro might want from me. I knelt with my bowl and slowly ate my dumplings. If I could not figure out what the Snake was planning, I would surely not come out the victor in his plans.

"You seem quieter today…"

I choked on the dough, having forgotten Xael was there. "Strategizing. Do you want to learn how to punch?"

Xael's eyes lit, effectively distracted. "Is that ok? I mean, am I allowed?"

I laughed. "I dictate what is allowed, and it isn't fitting for my guard to have no martial ability."

Xael was a diligent student—patient beyond his years and earnest beyond belief. All too soon, the moon rose and seven palanquins lined the cobbled stone street in front of the pagoda. We would be paraded to the palace steps for the grandest ball of the decade. Though invaluable, the event postponed my victories by another night.

I brushed the wrinkles off Xael's pressed uniform and asked, "Do you know how to wield a katana?"

"Captain Chiyo says I'm not ready to wield one in combat," he said with his head dipped, "but I can use the smaller one."

I laughed at that. The "smaller one" was known as a *wakizashi*, and it was a backup blade in battle.

"You'll grow into it," I reassured, passing my ornate *wakizashi* into his hands. Master Hito had taken me to the finest sword craftsman in Xinyue to help the smith make a perfect katana and wakizashi set for me. He left me with the smith for months during the painstaking process, but the result was beautiful. The sheath was a deeper black than the darkest night, with flakes of silver that sparkled like stars.

Strapping it to his belt, Xael asked, "How come there aren't any fights tonight?"

I blinked at him. He searched himself and the short sword's sheath. "What? What did I do?"

"You're not just new to the Dragon lineage, are you?" I realized. He shifted uncomfortably as his eyes bounced anywhere away from mine. "I will answer yours if you answer mine. How did you come to the Western Fortress?"

He pivoted his toe on the wood floor. "I came from a small set of islands in the southern waters."

"But what drove you to my fortress?"

Xael clenched his eyes shut and balled his fists. When his eyes opened, they had a shimmering grit. A challenging tone undercut his voice. "For a couple of years, Westerners overtook our villages. My father said it was the Dragon lineage's fault for abandoning us. I had to see for myself, so I climbed. Captain Chiyo appeared out of nowhere when I reached the top… That's why she knew she could send me down the cliff."

"That was the last excursion we went on together," I mused.

Master Hito left me in charge of the strategy which I soundly overcomplicated. When we arrived, all of my plans proved unnecessary. Xael's people were ready to fight, and the Westerners were tired of jungle living. One decisive victory sent them running.

Though they needed our help, Xael's people proved fearsome on the battlefield, navigating the vines and heavy brush like nothing I had ever seen. They appeared and began slaughtering the Westerners before they had any chance to react. If his people had more abundant and better resources, they wouldn't have needed us at all.

His father was right, in a way, to blame us. After all, it was an embarrassment that Xinyue had to send two master lineages to claim the tiny islands as ours. The emperor later banned many of their weapons, leaving them vulnerable to a Western attack.

This set Xael apart from me. He came from a people prided on their ferocity and skill with tools used for carnage. I came from nomads who roamed and traded within the safety of another people's borders. When they fell, my people didn't so much as hold up a finger.

It made sense how he learned to climb and travel with such ease. But how did a boy from such adept warriors come to lack even a hint of martial training? Xael studied me, waiting for a reaction. I tucked my questions away out of respect for our deal, and a sense that our time was running short.

I finally responded, "We don't fight tonight because it is a sacred night. Once a decade, the full moon shines so brightly, it leaves the impression of a second moon. That is the real reason for this festival. The duels are little more than a show to honor the occasion and an excuse to let the people see the lineages be ranked by skill."

"Why do the heirs fight instead of the masters?" he asked.

"Hm," I paused, thinking about how to explain what I innately understood. "The masters' purpose is to set the empire up for success in the next generation. Their heirs are the testament to that purpose."

Xael still looked confused. "But the emperor can reorder the lineages even if you win?"

"Success is more than skill on the battlefield, but enough questions. We ought to be on time to at least one event this festival," I said with a lighthearted grin. "Go, take the place of one of the swordsmen by my palanquin. I will join you shortly."

He scurried off to his post.

One by one, masters and heirs stepped onto open palanquins carried by four finely dressed men, and guarded by armored swordsmen.

I stood alone at the end of the line. Envy crept into my thoughts as I watched the other heirs thrive in the shadows of their masters. Several of the heirs thought themselves ready to become masters by the way they stood shoulder to shoulder with their mentors. I never cared to overtake my master. Who would want the responsibility of waiting on a fickle emperor?

Kirima stood a head shorter than her master, modestly waving to a sea of onlookers. More people flooded to the metal barricades at the edge of the streets than had watched our matches.

Inside the coliseum, the onlookers expected a certain amount of personal space and privacy…all of whom would be inside the palace, awaiting our entrance to the court dance. Here, every person crammed as close to the streets as they could manage, sandwiched in front of the next person in line who wished to be even an inch closer to the master lineages.

As the lineages paraded toward the palace, a warm breeze passed through the summer air. I found myself mesmerized by the swinging lanterns, though their light was made useless in the luminescence of the moon. Curtains cascaded through the air like the court dance had already begun.

In the sway of one, something caught my attention. A bowman trained his arrow on the palanquin in front of mine.

I leapt aboard, shoving Kirima to the side. Master Feiyu hadn't so much as looked at me since his outburst last night and I knew this would not help my standing with him.

"What in the high moon—"

"The windows!" I interrupted.

Both Leopards' ears twitched as two arrows flew toward Kirima. Master Feiyu shifted in front of her and batted both into the wooden platform with his palm. They weren't the real threat and Kirima was not the target. A third arrow, as silent as the coming of dew, followed perfectly in the blind spot created by the first two.

I snapped into its path, squeezing my fist to meet the arrow with a vibration of force. It splintered on impact.

Chaos reigned as the crowd screamed a horrid screech.

Two more arrows struck the front porters, tipping the palanquin. The armored guards stood aghast. Useless, inexperienced excuses for warriors.

"Into the alley!" I shouted above the noise.

"I will not flee!" Master Feiyu roared. I growled in response, but he still had a reputation to uphold. I huffed through my nose. No time for arguments.

"Then make a triangle," I barked between dodging arrows. I pointed to two soldiers, "And you two hold the platform vertical!"

Out of nowhere, Xael hoisted a side.

An agonized roar pierced the crowd's screams. Someone had managed to hit the Tiger master. Master Feiyu made to move, but dropped to the ground, narrowly avoiding another crossing of arrows. They were targeting masters.

"Go," he bit out, nose flared in rage. I paused. Worry filled my chest for the pinned pair and my signet bearer. "Do not patronize me, boy. I said go!"

I clenched my teeth and tore through the sea of people, passing two abandoned palanquins. The Snake and Monkey were smart enough to flee. A knife sliced my sleeve, opening a gash on my forearm. I reached out, but the knife vanished. I caught myself stepping after him. I couldn't be sucked into a chase right now; the battle raged ahead.

I caught sight of the Monkeys swinging into one of the buildings. If anyone could pin these guys down, it would be them. I dodged another swipe of a sinisterly curved knife. The Rhinos were still standing, heads above the rest. Neither paid heed to the arrows lodged in their tough skin, hardened through years of training much like my own.

Another blade appeared in front of me. I clamped onto the hilt, redirecting it just as the sword nicked my side. With an ear-splitting battle cry, I ripped through the crowd. Though the ghost of a man had vanished, I found my destination.

Baihu defended his fallen master's body from an onslaught of arrows and spears. I focused on my hands and cleaved several spears with a single swipe of my claws—no hiding this *qi* ability now. The warriors once holding the spears disappeared like specters in the morning light.

"That keeps happening," Baihu said, snapping an arrow in his hands. He lunged at a pair of swordsmen, snapping one's wrist and stabbing the other with his comrade's blade. Both vanished. He bellowed a furious cry. I spun my back against Baihu's and, with three blocks, shattered a trifecta of arrows.

A hand snatched mine from the side and tingles crawled up my arm. I opened my hand to block an incoming arrow, but it phased through my hand and impaled my shoulder.

"Ah!"

As fast as it appeared, the hand was gone. I snapped the end off of the arrow and searched for the fiend who shot it. I locked gazes with burning red eyes. The assassin, Lera, put a finger to her lips and faded away. Her arm was healed. That's what Pochi had meant. Sometimes I was so stupid!

As the panicked people dissipated, so did the attackers. The ground rumbled as the Rhino master fell to the cobblestone road.

Master Rohak's skin had grown thicker like a rhino's but it hadn't mattered. I looked at my uninjured hand, the one the arrow had phased through, and realized, they had likely done the same to him, despite his supernatural abilities.

I peeled my eyes away and looked at the Tiger master at my feet. His wounds were grave and his breathing agonal, yet he looked more promising than Master Rohak's still form, a handful of meters away.

"Master! Master Kabir!" Baihu cried from the fallen Tiger's side. A stab of guilt panged in my gut for the envy I felt moments ago.

The Qilin master approached from an alley while Zimo moved toward the Rhinos.

"Let me see," Master Kashvi said softly, subtly placing a hand on Baihu and me as she passed.

I snatched the head of the arrow from my shoulder with a grunt as the skin started to close around it. The gaping wounds had sealed by the time her knee set to the ground. She hummed, resting a hand on Master Kabir's pierced chest, and tapping her middle finger to his forehead. As she pulled away, the wound was gone though his eyes remained shut.

"Will he be okay?" Baihu asked. His jaw tensed and his foot fidgeted back and forth.

"Now he must fight his way back," she solemnly replied.

Baihu helplessly watched the rise and fall of his Master's chest. Pain pricked at my heart for him. I had felt the same help-less misery as I watched Pochi's life flicker out.

"Can't you do more?" Baihu asked.

"I am sorry, young cub," she said, her creases deepening in sorrow. "He is a strong warrior—believe in him."

Baihu bowed his head to the ground and prayed, "Follow the moon home; there are greater battles ahead."

The Qilin answered Zimo's beckon. I watched helplessly as she assessed Master Rohak's wounds. Her shoulders sank. Wisps of her hair caught in the wind as she shook her head.

"You!" Jai bellowed with a pointed finger. "You brought this misfortune!"

"Unless the teachings have changed, dragons bring good fortune," I snapped back. Of course they blamed me; it was the most convenient explanation. I looked to the Leopards for support. I saved Master Feiyu's life, but I was met with stony silence. I disgraced their lineage, they forsook mine—I supposed that made us even.

"Fine," I said raising my hands, "But this was the work of assassins."

"Assassins?" the Monkey master said, landing from the roof with Mehnaz. He clicked his teeth several times. "No…they disappeared from my grip. These were specters."

"Foolish superstition, Master Patish." An aged, thin man approached, followed closely by Shintaro. "Specters are simple stories to keep children in bed."

"Nice of you to finally join us, Master Isamu," Master Feiyu said softly.

"Perhaps," the snake master said with a nod to anxious onlookers peeking from windows, "The street is not the best place to deliberate."

Tension pulled tight like the strings of a violin. I coiled my fist, ready to strike the sword-bearing warrior who cleared his throat at my side. I let out a sigh and relaxed, realizing it was just Xael.

"I, um, swiped this," he said, handing me a deeply curved sword with an ornate hilt. "While they were focused on the Leopard master."

"Well done," I remarked, strapping it around my waist, "Very well done."

"Shall we continue to the palace," Master Kashvi suggested. "We cannot let whatever this was diminish our offerings to the emperor."

"You expect us to attend the court dance at a time like this?" Baihu protested. Jai nodded in agreement.

"It is not just a dance, it is a decennial tradition," Master Kashvi's voice grew stern.

"Forgive their statements of grief," Kirima spoke for them.

The Snake master affirmed, "We would, of course, be honored to celebrate the great moon in the palace."

The Qilin softened as she said, "This is a grievous time, but we are the empire's representatives. We must keep that in mind, especially in our darkest hours."

Nobles always had a part to play, even during the darkest hour on the brightest night.

The palace was as stunning as the first time I had set foot inside it. Tiles of white and blue ceramic patterned the floor. Paintings from every era and people group hung proudly between the sleek, sapphire columns that extended beyond sight. Truly, no empire compared to Xinyue.

Master Kashvi led us to two massive, ornate doors, decorated with squares of various precious stones and outlined by cords of silver.

"Welcome to the emperor's new court," she said, as two swordsmen heaved the doors open.

"Whoooah," awe slipped from Xael's mouth before he smacked a hand over it.

The chamber looked twice the size of the last rendition, neither of which had spared expense. Diamond windows lined the onyx walls that reached to the sky. The ceiling was as black as the night, with one glass circle for the double moon to shine through. On any other night, they would need as many torches as windows, but this night, the glass fragmented the moonlight to multiply the brilliant white orbs across the deep black walls. The marble floors further reflected the moonlight, illuminating the extravagant court.

"Now entering, the Dragon heir," a man proclaimed.

I held my chin high as I entered the court, and asked the first familiar noblewoman I saw to dance. Somehow, Baihu had found a partner with notable skill. They spun and swayed with each other like a willow on a late summer's eve. The graceful dance he chose contrasted with the brutal intensity of his fighting style.

"I'm sorry." My partner shook her head and stepped off of my toe. I looked into her deep brown eyes for the first time, ashamed I had paid her so little attention. Though Master Hito drilled formal dances into me like any other form, it had never held my interest. That wasn't fair to this woman, who was trying to make her family proud.

"Not at all," I said. "No one is watching us anyway. There's nothing to fear."

"She is." The young woman's eyes flicked behind me. "The Leopard heir."

I stepped back, as though presenting a masterpiece, and led her in a slow, smooth circle. One foot landed for every pluck of the *guzheng*. As we turned to circle again, her shoulders relaxed and her eyes twinkled.

"It's like moving with water," she said.

"From stone to stone on a riverbed," I agreed, closing the distance between us. "Until you reach the other side."

She brushed her fingers up my cheeks as I raised her arms and spun her gently to the end of the rhythm.

I bowed with her curtsy and led her back to her father's side. In a sea of onlookers, he was of the notable few who looked pleased with my victories.

"Thank you for lending her, Lord Jing," I said.

"Thank you for getting her feet to move," he chuckled. "You may be the first Mei has ever adhered to on a dance floor." The girl's cheeks flushed pink.

"Nonsense, she's a beautiful dancer. I must just be the first to make her feel the dance."

The man's chin tilted upward. "When you go searching for a bride—"

Mei tugged her father's sleeve, unable to bear the embarrassment any longer.

"I have much to accomplish before that time," I said, "Don't keep her waiting on a man's ambitions."

"Well, the offer stands," he said.

"Tell me, Lord Jing," I began, knowing the answer, "did I leave with any outstanding debts to you?"

"If anything, you left me in excess," he chuckled. "It turns out that when your broom boy becomes the Dragon heir, your swords become high in demand."

I grinned. "Yes, I suppose they would… Speaking of swords, do you know which manor makes ones like this?" I gently pulled the long blade from its sheath.

He hummed, inspecting it. "I'm afraid this isn't Xinyuan."

My face scrunched. "What do you mean?"

"It is not branded as any of the sword guilds', which means either it is foreign or one of the conquered are illegally smithing swords. And odd ones, at that."

"Thank you," I said, returning the sword to the titanium sheath. None of the conquered I had seen wielded such deeply curved blades. It resembled the Western cutlass, but it was too long. Why would a Western assassin be targeting a forsaken heir anyway? And how would a troop of them seamlessly stow away to assault the parade?

I dipped into a bow and searched the room for the others. Jai and Master Feiyu had both stepped aside as a group of nobles joined the floor. Xael stood exactly where I left him, attention caught by the table of fruits and pastries.

I caught Kirima staring at me. Her cheeks burned pink.

"It must be hard," I said as I approached.

"What?" she asked, refusing to look at me. "Watching everyone pretend everything is fine?"

"No, that is just the way of nobles." I paused out of respect for Master Rohak's absence. "I meant being a female heir. No man is brave enough to face your rejection and it would be an indiscretion for you to ask for a dance."

"I don't want to dance at a time like this." She shrugged, unconvincingly averting her eyes to Baihu and his partner. "It must be hard having every girl you dance with wanting to marry you."

I laughed and ran a hand through my ruffled hair. "Is that what you're afraid of?"

"Afraid of?" she gasped. "I'm not afraid of your—your—"

"My what?" I smirked, offering her my hand. "My sway?"

Kirima snatched it and stormed onto the floor as the next song began. The music thrummed and plucked like a building monsoon, thundering on the ground, and tinging against a tin roof. I stepped to her and she to me.

"That's not traditional," I teased, sweeping around her.

Kirima spun, her war dress growing with each twirl. "Does that frighten you?"

As the music drifted for a lull, I put my arm around her waist and slowed her spin to a stop. I looked into her focused eyes, inches from mine in the quiet. I whispered, "Not at all."

She whispered back, "I hope you know how to sword dance."

The music began in a sonorous deluge as she put her hand to my gut and slipped away with my new sword. She spun it between us, a dare in her eyes. I opened my arms wide, accepting the challenge.

Kirima thrust the sword to the thrums of percussion. I slid from one side to the other, relishing the nearness of the blade, and seeing just how close I could get. The music built like a flash flood, as did the complexity of Kirima's steps. I waited until I understood the motions.

Grief and anger mixed with aspiration as she stepped, stabbed, and swiped. I waltzed with her pain, side-stepping and ducking beneath the swipe with a sweeping leg. She shot her foot above my sweep, toes pointed perfectly to the moon. Kirima spun and dropped to a low stance as she switched to a reverse grip on the blade hidden behind her, mysterious and deadly.

I wanted wholeheartedly to know her more, and in this moment, nothing was stopping me. A step forward and she twirled away, waving her sword in warning. Another step and she bent over backward, creating a waterfall of fabric. One more step and she was to the edge of the dance floor. My heart clutched the air in my lungs as I forced her decision with one last step.

I gripped my sheath and angled it to her thrust, slipping the sword into the shimmering alloy. She sucked in a sharp breath as it clicked against her hip, matching a pause in the music. Eye to eye, the world stood still for us. Her blue eyes, which others called a cold defect, struck me in the luminescence as something wondrous and indomitable.

From the corner of my eye, I could see a heavy drumbeat falling. I shot my free hand past Kirima's head, circling it back as if to cup her neck which she bobbed beneath just enough to brush my forearm on the way back up.

The thrum came and I kicked the bottom of the sheath with the back of my heel, shooting the sword into the air. With another thrum, I swiped the sword at her legs. She twirled a kick just above my head—once, twice, three times.

Three beats and I caught her leg, cradling it atop my shoulder. She wrapped her leg around my arm and used the momentum to fan over my shoulder, as easily as the wind rolls over the hills, followed closely by my sword.

The final thrum reverberated. I stopped my sword, tip to the moon. Over my shoulder, I could see Kirima poised and facing the sky, a steady rise and fall to her shoulders. Kirima fell in step with me. Arm in arm, I escorted her to the outskirts of the dance floor. Somehow, I hadn't realized we were the only ones left.

"Everyone is watching," she whispered, confidence shaken.

"As they always will," I said. "Just as our masters stand above the rest, so will we."

"So cavalier," she said.

"You must be rubbing off on me." Kirima jutted her elbow into my side.

The announcer stepped to his calling point. "Now entering, the emperor!"

With swordsmen to either side, the emperor glided down the stairs from the black sky. His fawn skin paled in the cascading white light. An attendant swept in front of the procession. It would be a shame if any flecks of dirt soiled the perfectly white robes, decorated with golden animals chasing each other at the hem. I clenched my jaw. Was that all the lineages were to him? Animals playing at his feet? Those perfectly unblemished hands merely pointed and received while we toiled for his young dreams. I once believed they were dreams for the empire. With whitened knuckles, I couldn't help but question the teaching.

As Emperor Xinya reached his throne, imperial dancers took the floor as a new, enchanting tune plucked to life. A handful pointed their toes perfectly to the high moon and spun like a perfectly balanced top while the others twirled, swooped, and leapt weightlessly through the air. The fabric of their dresses, purples and yellows no commoner would ever touch, flapped brilliantly. Their synchronized and impossible movements awed the audience. Ten minutes ago, it might have impressed me too. In their perfection, they lost their passion—you could see it in their set expressions.

One by one, the lineages bowed before the young emperor and offered their gifts. Ancient discoveries, precious stones, and expensive tapestries were his favorites. I called Xael to my side, a smudge of powder on his cheek. I retrieved the giant bloodstone from the pack he held. Master Hito had instructed me to take the jade, but that said too little. Bloodstone matched the empire's lucky colors, with a deep red like the blood spilled to garner it. This empire was won with blood that we spilled for it—no, for the emperor. I bowed at the emperor's feet, face to the ground with both hands extended as they barely cradled the stone.

"Please accept this gift," I said.

I could hear a smile in his voice as he said, "I have never seen such a large blood jewel. This pleases me." His attendant hefted the gem from my hands, freeing me to rise.

"Sanav, is it?"

I paused, one knee still on the ground, and compacted the growing rage. It swelled in my blood, tingling my skin and provoking my response. Something deep and primordial cried out for the emperor's blood. I forced a slow, seething breath.

"At your service, Emperor Xinya."

"Where did you acquire that odd blade?" he asked.

"It was taken from an assailant this night," I answered, affectless.

His eyes fixed sharply on the sword. "It would delight me to add it to my collection."

A suspicion budded in my mind. Could he have ordered the massacre or was that theory just a convenient excuse to kill him?

"It is and always was yours, Emperor," I said, unstrapping the sheath and handing it to the attendant dressed in pure white silk that lustered under the full moon. The emperor's eyes clung to the curved blade. I shrewdly watched him evaluate it. A mere three decades, and yet his hair was already speckled with salt. "May it be put to good use at your charge."

He snapped a grave look at me. *Do something about it,* my squared shoulders dared. He said nothing as I bowed. *Coward,* I thought as I returned to my place among the nobles. The emperor had no special power, no godly insight. He had nothing I could not match.

I surveyed the remaining masters, catching sight of Master Feiyu just as he disappeared. The room moved as if nothing had changed. The doors did not open, the lineages continued to mingle with the nobles. He could be anywhere watching, but where would he wish to be most?

I ascended the staircase to the roof outlook. Crisp air graced my lungs atop the glass ceiling. The night was quiet as most of the populous hunkered in their homes. The nobles feared the emperor more than whatever force they believed had come against us. Somehow, the lineages had to handle both the emperor's wishes and the assassins' threat.

"Stuffy in there," I baited the Leopard master to appear.

From the ground, the roof was black, but from above it was merely tinted glass. I could see all of the people dancing and talking like beetles at my feet. The emperor had been watching us enter from up here. He had seen our dances and conversations like a fly on the wall. Master Feiyu appeared on the edge of the stonework, nearest the city. He stood like a gargoyle sentry with no indication of breath or life.

"You and Kirima seemed anything but stifled," he said with a voice that seemed to be carried by the wind itself.

"I—I meant no disrespect," I said. In all honesty, I hadn't thought about him at all when I approached Kirima to dance.

"I have no issue with your friendship," he breathed. "I just ask that you consider her best interest as much as your master's."

I stood speechless. I shouldn't have even given the appearance that she was allied with me. I chose recklessness, and we both knew it would hurt her in the end. Then again, the Leopard left me out to dry in front of the other lineages a mere hour ago. Still, a vein of embarrassment heated the tips of my ears until I could bear the silence no longer.

"What are you doing up here?"

"Master Kashvi was right to keep up appearances, but time is of the essence," he said with his back to me. Halfway into the sky, wind whipped through his salt-and-pepper hair. Mysterious awe betrayed my anger toward him. What must it be like to be invisible? He had the power to watch anything he wished without anyone taking note. That power came with all the responsibility of hearing and seeing everything within the city, and yet he was only one man.

"You intend to chase ghosts?" I asked.

"Ghosts do not use swords. They are still out there and I intend to catch them. I cannot hunt while stuck inside the palace."

"It may be more possible than you think." I said, looking down on the dancing nobles.

He whispered harshly, turning from the torchlit city, "Have you lost your mind?"

"Why else would he want the sword?" I asked. "He's angry I haven't lost and taking it out on the other lineages."

"The emperor often collects items from the conquered people," he dismissed.

"But this blade is not from a conquered people," I retorted. "I don't know why, but he's trying to get rid of the Dragon lineage."

"I am not having this discussion. The emperor would not attack his lineages with foreigners or assassins. That is a ridiculous accusation," he said. "I will forget you even suggested it. I recommend you do the same."

"The edict Master Hito denied was to take our soldiers to the North at the end of summer—they wouldn't have survived," I argued.

Master Feiyu gaped at me. The Leopard fixed his eyes into a glare, boring them into me as if digging through my very soul. He could stare all he wished. I spoke the truth and I would never shy away from it. The emperor decided to end us through death or disgrace.

The door unlatched and Shintaro slithered onto the rooftop. His miry smirk bristled against my already agitated temper.

"Am I interrupting?" Shintaro asked, fully knowing he was.

"I was just leaving," the Leopard said, hopping into the night. He was wasting his time searching for trouble among the commoners.

"Are you second-guesssing?" Shintaro asked.

"Clearly my plans are garnering attention," I said.

"Yesss, indeed," he said with a simper. "Then the price of my sssilence is high."

I crossed my arms and asked, "What do you want, Shintaro?"

He circled, sliding his tongue across his upper lip. His fingers flicked toward me in an unnerving twitch. I had proven myself a better fighter than him and yet an ominous pang shot up my spine prodding for a reaction.

"In the ascension ritual, the strongest master is challenged last," he said. "And so the Dragon will challenge the Leopard first."

"Why?" What did the Snake gain from a forsaken lineage disgracing another lineage?

He smiled, "Let me worry about that. Tell Massster Hito to challenge the Leopard first and the Snake last, and I will ensure a smooth path for you."

Of course, it finally struck me. "Master Isamu wants more sway for something. More experiments?"

"You get your way, I get mine."

I shook my head. A simple 'yes' would have sufficed. The Dragon and Leopard had always restrained the Snake's voracious appetite for progress. One way or the other, the lineage of the Snake gained greatly if one of us lost the first ascension duel.

"Fine," I said. "I will ensure the Dragon master challenges the Leopard first."

A gasp chilled the air. My gut twisted as she flashed into view.

"Kirima, wait!" I called out as if I had anything good to say. It didn't matter; she was already descending the stairs. "You snake!"

I turned to grab Shintaro. He slipped through my grip like ox snot. He chuckled sadistically. "A witnesss ensures a contract."

"Her lineage's status is now on the line. What makes you think she won't have us both killed?" I snapped.

"I watch for weaknessses," he said. "You are hers."

I stormed back to the court dance. Kirima kept as much distance as humanly possible between us. I didn't know what to say anyway. What could I say? An apology wouldn't replace her master's status. Flustered, I accepted the distance, hoping Shintaro was right.

The dancing and false levity nauseated me to watch. I couldn't stand another awkward stumbling of a conversation nor the look of disdain from nobles who had no right to stand in my presence. This was all a great excuse for them. As one of the conquered, I never really had a place in this echelon. As my resentment grew, I decided to take my leave with Xael.

Jai's sudden climb to mastery of the Rhino art offset the pairings, but Master Kashvi's insistence that Baihu take a day to rest after valiantly defending his master leveled the matches for the next evening. That placed Kirima against Mehnaz and Shintaro against me to ensure all of the heirs competed against each other by the end of the week. It was high time I got my hands on that Snake.

Under the waning moon, Master Kashvi announced, "After the unfortunate events of last night, Emperor Xinya has decreed that the Dragon must make it abundantly clear that fortune is with him."

Hushed whispers filtered through the crowd. Would it be a new stipulation or challenge? "His opponents are now sanctioned to use lethal force." Gasps filled the air.

I smiled at the unbelievable verdict. Could he make it any clearer that he wanted me dead? Master Feiyu stared ahead blankly. How could he not see the obvious?

Kirima and Mehnaz took the stage. Their stances foretold the result. The Leopard crouched with a soft fist ready to strike. The Monkey hunkered with both fists planted on the ground.

The gong sounded and Mehnaz crashed into Kirima, who rolled with the force and sent Mehnaz flying over her. The Monkey skidded to her feet, another charge at the ready. This time she aimed for Kirima's hips. For a moment, I thought I was wrong about the matchup. Mehnaz's shoulder hit Kirima's hip and lifted. Kirima dug her elbows into Mehnaz's shoulders. The Monkey heir grunted and let go before finishing the throw.

As Kirima landed on one foot, the other knee pulled to her chest and snapped a devastating kick. The Monkey heir wobbled and fell.

"I hope you are prepared," I taunted Shintaro.

"I cannot wait," he returned.

Shintaro brushed his green uniform and patted the dust off his orange cloth shoes. The story goes that the Snake was the first assassin lineage before it was reformed by the Xinyue Empire and brought into the high seven. I questioned the legend's claim that the Snake was ever reformed.

At the gong's reverberation, I blasted across the distance. Shintaro coiled to the ground, a foolish strategy against the Dragon. Committed to the charge, I left both hands open to defend his strikes and swung a leg to kick him into motion. Shintaro's knees hit the ground just as I released the kick. He hastened to duck his forehead to the stone floor, narrowly avoiding the impact. As I pulled my foot back to stomp, Shintaro tapped the ground twice.

"Match!" Master Kashvi announced.

"What?" I yelled in deafening unison with Baihu.

"I yield," Shintaro hissed from his low bow. Even quieter he whispered, "Baihu's weakness is his full dedication in all things."

"Get up," I demanded. Slowly, he rose to his feet and bowed a supposed apology to the masters.

"What is the meaning of this," Master Kashvi called from her station.

"Master Kashvi," Shintaro said, "The victory was clear before the match started. There was no need to prolong my defeat." No one ever yielded before injury. A fighter could yield at any time, but in yielding before fighting, he shamed his lineage and his master. Why would he do that?

"If he refuses to fight, I will," Baihu proclaimed, advancing from the tunnel.

"I accept," I said, placing my flat hand against my fist and bowing.

Baihu shoved Shintaro out of the dueling position. He took a dipped position with most of his weight on the back leg and two uncurled hands, ready to maul me. Unlike the Leopard, he only had offensive positions. We both waited for Master Kashvi to sanction the duel. It was unusual for a duel to take place in the midst of the challenge of heirs, but we were set to fight tomorrow anyway. She swallowed, shook her head in disbelief, and signaled for the gong. The end was nearer than I imagined. Victory called my name.

I met Baihu in the middle. I dodged his grasp at my head

and jutted my knee at him. He side-stepped and nailed a backfist across my cheek. I rotated away from him and arced a spinning heel kick into his ribcage. Baihu's face contorted into a grimace as he retreated to catch his breath.

The crowd of onlookers was silent. Not even murmurs reached in from the streets beyond.

"There's no shame in admitting you've been bested," I said.

"Quiet, serpent," he growled, regaining his composure.

I wiped the pain from my jaw and readied for the next exchange. I let Baihu make the first move. He charged, leaping over my sweep with a flying side kick. I sidestepped the attack, only to be caught in his claws as he spun midair. As he landed, Baihu ripped me into his knee.

Pain stabbed up my center. I grunted but it didn't stop me from grabbing Baihu and anchoring my feet back to the ground.

We clasped shoulders in a standoff. He kicked out my knee as I scissored his elbow between the blades of my forearms. Even losing my balance, I could feel the break as his joint popped against my forearm. Baihu grunted away the pain with inhuman grit.

I tried to recover my balance, but he toppled me with his good arm. I took the momentum into a roll that carried me to my feet, with Baihu hot on my trail. He only had one hand to defend, so his strikes would deviate to kicks and counters. Or so I thought, before a hook punch sailed toward my jaw. I guarded with my right and hooked into his broken elbow with the other.

His yowl struck me with guilt. He was in my way, but that didn't mean he deserved such targeting. But didn't he? He left my master out to dry. They all did! Was I really sympathizing with my adversary at a time like this? They all deserved exactly what they were given.

Baihu cupped the back of my neck, pulling me into a knee. I tensed to rebuff the blow and land an elbow across his unguarded face. Blood streamed from his brow. With a blind eye, broken elbow, and cracked ribs, he had clearly lost.

As I feinted another jab to his elbow, he drilled a tiger fist into my sternum. I wheezed against the cracked cartilage and stumbled back, stunned. He had completely abandoned his injuries. He knew he lost; he was just hell-bent on taking me with him. I saw it in his predatory snarl now. The regal, upstanding heir I knew had melted away. Only a feral tiger remained. Lethal force was forbidden for me—how could I put him down without killing him?

Bloodlust dripped from Baihu as he bolted from a crouch. He grabbed for my throat to distract from his stomp coming to my foot. I batted away the grab and cupped the back of his foot with mine just before it landed. With the slightest yank, he dropped into a full split, immediately beginning a swirling whirlwind kick on his back that scissored my legs from under me. I grimaced on the descent as our fists simultaneously met. My protruding knuckle completely shattered his hand. I felt it sink and splinter his bones through the skin. His roar stole the breath from everyone in the coliseum.

I landed on him, pinning his arms. His legs cinched around my waist, painfully constricting my diaphragm.

I looked to Master Kashvi for a pleading second. Whatever her orders were from the emperor, surely she could see Baihu digging his own grave. A tear fell from her cheek even as she shook her head at me.

Baihu slammed his head into mine while I was distracted. Blood streamed over my left eye. He tried again, making room for me to slip both arms behind his head. He had no force, no escape, but I had no leverage.

"Yield, dammit—Just yield!" I screamed.

"Never!" he shouted. His yell splattered blood across my ear.

I released his arms to dig both elbows into his thighs, raking until they released me. He curled up to elbow my gut and flung his arms around my waist with a feral battle cry. I hugged his neck and pressed with every bit of anger and sorrow I had left to fuel me. There was no reason good enough to put an imperial warrior through this. I didn't deserve it and neither did Baihu. He blasted my ribs with his good elbow over and over. His pain had to be enormous. I cried out my frustration, constricting until he fell limp.

As Master Kashvi hurried to the center, I shouted for everyone to hear, "I am ready for the emperor's call."

Without so much as a look at the masters who agreed to this savagery, I stormed down the tunnel.

Xael was sewing the last stitch into my forehead when a knock came on my door. He flipped the string and tied the knot, nodding in approval of his work. He had done well by my side. I couldn't admit it, but I would miss him. I patted his shoulder and walked to the bamboo door.

"Yes?" I opened the door to an unexpected visitor. I ushered the elder heir into the room and signaled for Xael to close the window. "Zimo?"

"Have you sent for Master Hito?" he asked.

"No, not yet," I said. Zimo closed the door and surveyed the room.

"The emperor will hear the Dragon's case tomorrow night. He will need to appear at the palace steps before the moon rises." Zimo's brisk tone sent a shiver up my spine. He was not a gruff man but his tone was grim.

"Is there something wrong?"

His foot tapped impatiently. "It was just a brutal display tonight."

His eyes shifted in a way far more characteristic of Shintaro than of the Qilin heir. "Now that the competition is over for you, I can see to your injuries."

I eyed him suspiciously. I still didn't know why Master Kashvi healed me after the parade and his anxiousness set me on edge.

"I'd rather you didn't," I said, taking a quarter step back.

His mouth parted, closed, and then he said, "Wh—you don't want healing?" His hand twitched uncomfortably.

My eyebrows creased in concentration on the Qilin. "The emperor has disowned my lineage. Until that is reversed, I have no claim to the empire's resources, and it has no claim on me."

"I—I see… If that is how you see it." He shifted from heel to heel.

If I could catch anyone in a lie it would be the most innocent heir who had seen neither war nor conquest. "I know the emperor hired the assassins, Zimo. I know he wants to be rid of the Dragon's legacy enough to release outlaws on the lineages."

"That's not true," he defended too quickly. "The emperor would never disown the Dragon without reason."

"I would love to hear the reason," I said, arms wide open. He closed his eyes and turned his head away. "Tell the emperor the Dragon will answer his call tomorrow."

For the last time.

"He will come in time?" he asked, eyes wide on me.

"He will."

Zimo exited quickly and quietly. I lightly dragged my finger across the thin stitching that held my skin together. I knew rest would do me well, but I was so close to the end.

I could already see the shock on the emperor's face.

The awe in the people's eyes.

The world at my fingertips.

I flopped my head down on my cot and huffed.

"Not yet," I reminded myself. My muscles melted, craving their well-earned respite.

My mind was not so still. That same dream haunted my slumber.

"I made a mistake," Master Hito said, far too late to redirect my swing. Time froze as our eyes locked. His intensity burned into my soul. Had I finally broken through to him? He finally saw this was not the only way, but it was too late. There had to be something I could do!

I lopped his draconic head clean off his deformed body, disgracing him. Both sloughed to the ground like rotten husks. I stood in disbelief and oppressive guilt. The dragon head lay still on its side. I was only supposed to sever the spine. In my haste to end his suffering, I had shamed us both. Its eyes blinked away the glazed death and locked sideways with mine.

"But it's not too late for you."

I sat up on my bedroll, heaving several breaths. Breathing no longer pinched my sternum and the room was clear and shaded. I reached up to the window and popped it open as I had done time and time again. The sun shone brilliantly in the sky. What must it be like to be untouchable and yet never as revered as the moon?

"Oh," Xael said, sliding into the room, "It didn't seem like you would wake soon."

"Hm? I should have been awake hours ago," I said, still entranced by the blinding light.

"You were tired, but gaining strength steadily," he said. "I brought lunch. Pork slices on rice."

"Thank you," I took the bowl. Steam swam into the air, filling the room with tantalizing fragrance. "You have done well."

"It's just lunch." He shrugged.

"I mean all of it," I said, sincerity coating my words. "You can return to our stronghold proud. Tell Captain Chiyo I send you with my highest esteem."

"You're not…you can't send me back now." A crease set between his dark eyebrows.

"When I meet with Emperor Xinya, I will claim preeminence," I explained, "If I succeed, I will be in the highest esteem in the empire, even above the emperor. If I fail, I will be a blasphemous heretic—and so will you if you come with."

Xael's dark eyes flitted from side to side trying to integrate the information. His shoulders squared and his chest puffed out. The crease never left his forehead and I could see a fight in his eyes.

"Then I haven't completed my task."

"Xael," I rumbled.

"Master San." He took a defiant step. "Captain Chiyo sent me to shadow you until the festival is over. Punish me for my orders if you have to, but I will complete them."

I scanned the boy for any sign of exploitable hesitance, but all

I found was resignation in his saddened eyes. This had nothing to do with orders. His face scrunched, his eyes and his mouth set in a straight line, but his hands vibrated.

"Don't you understand what I'm saying?" I grabbed his shoulders firmly. "If I fail, they will kill us both."

"You won't lose," he said, his legs now quaking too.

It finally clicked. "You believe I've already lost, don't you?"

Twice now, my tunnel vision clouded my thinking. I should have seen this sooner and I should have seen Shintaro's plot at the onset.

"I…no…I just…"

"Spit it out."

"Your energy hasn't transformed yet," he mumbled, barely audibly.

"You mean it doesn't look like the other masters'." I pulled a finger under his chin. "Right?"

He swallowed. "It hasn't shaped itself yet. You're close, but you're not there. I thought you might last night…but then you woke up."

Vexed, I snapped, "It will have to be close enough."

"It can't hurt to let me come," Xael pleaded.

"It could kill you, actually," I said. "Especially if your assessment is correct." But it was the only hope I had left. It was too late for me to alter my course. If this was my fate, I could join Master Hito as his loyal heir.

"I can help," Xael finally blurted as if a final barter. "If you let me come, I can read their *qi*."

"You haven't done that already?"

"It's different right before combat," he explained with an extended hand. "It stills in a different way when it's being prepared. I don't know how to explain it, but I'm telling the truth."

"Master Hito never mentioned any of this."

He said, "It's a secret among inheritors, or masters, as you say."

"Hm," I hummed with crossed arms. There was something else to this, but Xael squirmed as if he had already said too much. He wouldn't be saying any more without harsher tactics. "Ok, Xael. You can stay, but if it becomes apparent I've lost, you will flee."

He paused, evaluating the bargain. "Fine."

We clasped forearms to seal it.

17

Night fell as I stood in front of the palace gate, Xael faithfully at my side. Master Hito's belt, passed from master to heir for generations, was cinched at my waist. It was once a deep red, but years of experience seeped the blood from its victories. It filled me with pride to call it my own.

Several guards hoisted the bronze chains that controlled the gate. Each step toward the emperor's throne spurred my heart to beat faster. My eyes narrowed on the gaudy doors to the emperor's court. My purpose would finally be complete.

The drums of war beat against my heart as I stepped into the chamber lined with swordsmen. Columns of marble lined the outer edges, creating an almost hall-like effect in the massive throne room. I pressed into center stage, where marble floors swirled with black and white, like the intermixing of yin and yang. Not a soul stood between me and Emperor Xinya, who sat upon his heightened gold throne with a glass of wine, peering down at me. One leg folded over the other, revealing his feet, adorned in golden sandals. His long fingers splayed toward the floor in front of him, inviting me to bow and begin our discussion. The thought sickened me. As I strode closer, his head tilted to the side.

"Where is my Dragon master?" he asked, halting my steps. *His* Dragon master?

"I am the Dragon master, Emperor."

He surveyed me, beginning at my feet and pausing at my belt. His mouth dipped at the edges the longer his hazel eyes lingered.

"So it seems. And you have come… To what end?" His voice was silvery yet grating in my ears.

For all the trouble this man had caused me, I could kill him here and now. But that would only ensure Master Hito's name would remain marred forever. I had to shine brighter than the moon.

"I declare preeminence," I boomed, death in my veins.

His glass of wine shattered to the ground in a spray of red mist. The royal guards stepped to draw their swords but froze at the emperor's call. In unison, they stepped back into attention.

"Don't be a fool," the emperor said. "You would be better following my edicts."

"The edicts that hired an assassin to kill me?" I accused, voice charged with venom. "Your edicts to kill all of my men? Your edicts to eradicate Master Rohak and Kabir?"

"Enough!" He shouted on his feet. "You speak heresy in my court?"

I took a defiant step toward him. "I am preeminent in your courtroom! Call on your lineages and I will ascend!"

Shintaro and Master Isamu were the first to slither into the room from the rooftop, followed by Master Kashvi and Zimo. Runners retrieved the others as we stood in stony silence. Eyes like daggers, I watched the other lineages file into the room. Hostility rushed from them like a tsunami. It met a stone wall. I finally had everything where I wanted it.

"You believe these, your peers and elders, to be below you?" Emperor Xinya asked, fanning their anger toward me.

I stuck my nose up like I had seen Baihu do so many times before. Their anger would only hasten my victories. "I have already proved these so-called peers are beneath my skill."

"You filthy—" Baihu began.

"Silence! You had your chance," the emperor commanded. "It is convenient that you choose now to claim preeminence when two masters have fallen."

"Was it not you who said fortune would have to be on my side to prevail?" I goaded with an implicit accusation. Fortune would have to be on my side because he wasn't. He caused these deaths, this upheaval. He forced my hand.

Puffing his chest, the emperor said, "If you believe you know so much, you should know you will have to face my royal guard before challenging the masters."

"I accept this," I said. Xael tugged my sleeve lightly. I dipped to his height.

"The furthest two have too much qi," he whispered.

I nodded and took my place in the center of fifteen royal guards without so much as a dagger to defend myself. They were clad in armor and sharpened helmets and very other guard had a face piece reminiscent of the demons in my nightmares. Most leaned toward me, confident in their armored shoulder plates and bronze, lamellar breastplates. Their time would come. My priority was those reluctant to fight. Their swords rested at their sides. For most, this would be a death sentence, but I would make it a spectacle.

"Draw!" the emperor ordered. The sounds of war reverberated in my ears as metal slid into action. "Begin!"

"Make an example of the unprepared assailants," Master Hito had taught me. The circle steadily closed around me until each guard was one step from having my head with their long, straight swords.

Too easy, I thought as I found my first targets. Two guards stood side by side, lagging just a hair behind the others. The guards raised a leg in unison, this time with blades high and ready to split me into thin slices.

I slammed into the two guards with shaky hands and death grips on their swords. They clattered to the ground, the least of my worries. I swiveled through the opening as two swords plummeted toward me. I led one into the guard scrambling to his feet.

I dropped and swept the other guard off his feet. I stepped across the hands on the floor, feeling the crunch that made sure they would not be able to strike me from behind, and then I moved to the next warrior. He too met a fateful collision as I completely outmaneuvered the sword's speed and crashed my fist into his unguarded face.

The first two I toppled were just getting back to their feet as the next swordsman hurled his sword at me like a javelin. Fool. I shifted just to the left, letting it sail into the guard hoping to end me from the rear. His scream gave me all the information I needed. I pressed on.

Without a sword, the soldier hopelessly defended my assault. *A man that needs a sword will always bow to one who needs only himself.* I controlled his movements, putting him in the way of a blade meant for me. His cry was quickly joined by his backstabber's as I snapped her extended arm.

Several more guards decided a joint attack was their best hope, learning nothing from their comrades' fates. I ripped the helmet off my last victim and hurled it at the coming guards. They blocked with their swords, buying me the time to lock one's swing above his head while I kicked another's knee sideways. I felt it pop and turned, sending a back kick into another's charge.

The soldier I pinned tried to free his sword hand by pulling it further back, giving me momentum to topple him straight onto his back. I kicked the sword just before he would have fallen on it and crashed a knee into his helm.

The remaining royal guards edged closer cautiously. The center one adjusted her grip as the wingmen charged. I sidestepped and left one leg out to trip, but both jumped in time. The next two came with perfectly synchronized thrusts. I stumbled back, inhaled, and let out a breath of fire.

"Impossible!" Master Patish gasped. The guards fell, yelling and patting the burning cloth. The last two leapt over their burning comrades. I snapped toward the other two, while they awaited their cue. "Wait at the ready" I had learned early. Clearly, they still needed that lesson.

Their swords flailed. I disarmed one and used him as a shield against the other. The sword stabbed clean through his comrade and slit my side. The imp hadn't withheld his force at all when his comrade was placed in the way.

I turned my wrath toward the circling royal…guards? I had seen these two silhouettes before.

"Couldn't wait for a rematch?" I called to the woman with burnt orange eyes. Lera, the assassin, hid herself among the royal guards. I owed Xael my thanks for the warning about the extra qi.

She charged, earning a disapproving huff from her comrade. Lera dropped the sword and slipped a dagger into each hand. I rushed to meet her.

The world faded as everything finally fell into place. Revenge for Pochi and Master Hito was so close I could taste it. I could *feel* it like butterflies in my gut—the readiness to succeed. The readiness to end this assassin and ascend.

"Master!" Xael yelled, catching my attention just in time to drop beneath a blade meant for my neck. So caught in my thoughts, I had forgotten about the other assassin.

A quick circle step put both assassins in front of me. I blazed fire over them as hot as I could muster. Instead of screams, I was met with a swiping blade. I ducked and rammed a double palm strike into the man's hip. His knees buckled and his hands reached for my shoulders. I lifted the underside of his arm, spun around, and threw him over my shoulder. Empty gasps puffed from his lungs.

I dodged three throwing knives. Lera wanted to keep her distance. I shouldn't have been surprised that an assassin would be such a coward.

I charged, ducking, shifting, and passing knives as I advanced. As my time to react shrunk, several blades left nicks and marks. I raised my hand to deflect the last knife, but it phased right through my hand, implanting in my shoulder. I swore that would be the last time her ghostly effect would land. I tackled her to the ground, ripping off her helm. Blonde hair fanned above her head. With her mobility grounded, I pinned her arms and prepared a dragon's fist for her temple.

"She yields!" The man coughed behind me.

Her face twisted. "Luk—"

"My sister yields," he shouted over her.

I froze above her. He kidnapped Xael. She killed Pochi. They killed Master Rohak and might have killed Master Kabir. I could not forgive that even if no one else recognized these outlaws protected by the emperor. But this wasn't about me. It wasn't about them.

"You heard them, Dragon master," the emperor said. "You've earned your right to challenge."

I released her and stood. Xael rushed to my side with a bandage. He pulled out the knife, cut the wrapping, and pressed the cloth to my wound.

"Take it off," I instructed.

He gingerly removed the bandage. I sniffed and shot a tiny breath at the wound, cauterizing it. I winced as it sizzled to a stop. Xael insisted on wrapping it anyway. Emperor Xinya waved a hand to clear the injured from the room as he settled back into his throne.

The emperor asked, "So, who will it be?"

Jai was already stepping forward when I declared, "I will defeat the Leopard first."

"What?!" Master Feiyu roared. "You challenge me *first*?"

Kirima clenched her teeth, eyes watering a stream of resentment. I hated doing this to her. Was I any better than my peers who had willfully forsaken me for their own gain? I had to do this. I had to make things right. This was Shintaro's fault for cornering me into this deal. I despised the way his eyes gleamed, soaking in the tension. His time would come, I could be sure.

"Jai hardly counts as a master yet," I said, "You wouldn't subject him to a death duel without an heir, would you? I challenge the Leopard, Monkey, Rhino, and Snake to stop my ascension, should they dare."

Xael stood to the side, biting his bottom lip. He shouldn't have to watch this. I hoped I would be able to win without killing anyone, but I would be a fool to underestimate the masters. Anyone Master Hito regarded as a peer garnered my respect. Not to mention the possibility that I lost and Xael was forced to share in my punishment. Why would he risk his life to stay with me? All this time he walked faithfully at my side and I never knew why. My weakness was the same as Baihu's—too focused on putting my energy into one effort.

"It is just as you said," the emperor said to the Snake at his side. He had achieved more than the regard of a forsaken heir. How stupid could I be? I gave him the esteem of a prophetic strategist.

"You arrogant, misbegotten orphan," Master Feiyu seethed, taking to the courtroom floor.

"Wait for the shiver," Xael whispered, receding to the edge of the room.

As I took my place across from Master Feiyu, I felt a vibrating readiness overtake me. The emperor and his pets surrounded us, but the Leopard master was all I saw. If I came out victorious, no one could stand in my way. I funneled energy into my hands like the night of the parade. My fingers contorted into scaled claws capable of tearing through a person with one clean swipe. Dragon claws would claim my victory.

The leopard master sunk back defensively. He outstretched a hand and folded his fingers, daring me to charge. I stepped and froze. *Wait for the shiver,* echoed in my mind. What shiver? Everything stilled in the air as Leopard faced Dragon—the most formidable lineages. His eyes glazed with death while mine burned with an unquenchable fire. I dared an inch forward.

Ice shot through my spine like thousands of needles. My hair electrified the back of my neck as I whipped around to see the real Master Feiyu piercing the air with a knife-hand strike. I barely raised my clawed hands in time to block, merely scraping his skin in return. I stumbled a step as I took a deep breath. His eyes sparked in surprise, but he didn't dodge the flames. He didn't dodge because he wasn't there anymore. Another set of needles stabbed up my back. I was too late to block. With his curled fingers millimeters from my skin, I sent my qi to shield the attack, forming young scales at the impact site.

"No!" Xael shrieked to my right. He leaned toward me past the marble columns, gripping it until his entire arm trembled.

Master Feiyu's Leopard's paw padded into me with no force and now he couldn't dodge. I started to smile until I felt it. He sent a wave of his qi blasting into mine like an avalanche. I felt as if I had been forced from my body, flying into the back wall. Except, I crumpled.

No, I cried to myself. *Get back up!* My body hit the ground; the ceiling swam with lights and dragons. *You can't lose,* I berated myself, willing my eyes to stay open.

Master Feiyu loomed over me, casting a menacing shadow. His fuzzy figure hesitated.

They could say what they wanted, but I would die loyal to the man who raised me as his own. He trusted me with something he considered higher than his life, and I would be a coward to run from this end. Tingles filled my body, screaming for me to move. I could see the Leopard's fist plummeting toward me, but the paralysis anchored me in place. My eyes grew mercifully hazy as hallucinations overtook me; an ethereal, azure dragon wrapped its body around mine.

"No please!" Kirima gripped her master's arm. "Don't kill him!"

"He's a heretic and a blasphemer!" Master Feiyu peeled her off.

"What other choice did we give him?" she asked, as the haze consumed me.

I could have run—joined a legion and kept my head low. This was my decision, and my failure to bear.

19

I groaned like an old stairway as I forced myself onto an elbow. Every inch of my body ached and my head was nauseatingly fuzzy. The hallucinated dragon remained at the edge of my vision. Was this the beginning of my journey to the afterlife? The room was an exact replica of the mountain fortress when the clouds dipped and cast a deep fog over the lookout. I always loved its crisp air.

"Master San, you're finally awake," Captain Chiyo breathed in relief right behind me.

My head whipped around to see her, a thousand questions fighting to escape my mouth as my vision came in and out of focus. My sight sharpened around her but everything else blurred unrecognizably as I sat the rest of the way up. Captain Chiyo sat by my bed with her bronze helm set to one side and her katana strapped to the other. Her light beige features were proof of her dedication to her armor that protected her from sun and foe alike.

"How did I get here?" I asked, standing and quickly falling back to a knee. In all my training, I had never felt so weak. Something sickly crawled beneath my skin like a host of maggots inside a corpse.

"Xael brought you back to us," she said, her lilting accent carrying a grave tone.

"He couldn't have—he didn't bring a horse," I said.

She chuckled with a somber smile. "He wished for me to apologize on his behalf for stealing your pack and buying a horse."

"He can apologize himself," I said, wobbling onto my feet. Dizziness scratched the edges of my vision. At least if I died in the palace, the common soldiers would be spared. "He shouldn't have brought me here."

Her eyelids drooped, grief cast over her features. "He can't…"

"What do you mean?" I asked. If anyone had so much as touched him—

"He has yet to awake. When he arrived at the Eastern Cliff face, he abandoned the horse, tied you to himself and climbed."

"What?" I stumbled and Captain Chiyo caught my arm, slipping it over her shoulder. "That's…"

What words could do him justice?

"Extraordinary," she said with a sad smile. "He had trouble mixing with the other soldiers when he first came, but he has returned as a hero."

I didn't know whether to be thankful or angry with him. I warned him my life would be forfeited if I lost. He promised he would flee at the first sign of loss. I supposed neither mattered anymore. I did lose, and he did bring me back here. I lost royally in the first battle. Master Feiyu made a fool of me and perhaps I had earned it. Who was I to think I could accomplish more than my master believed me capable of?

I sighed, "Captain Chiyo, would you bring me my wakizashi?"

"Your sword, sir?" she asked.

"The price of failure," I said with a hard swallow.

"Xael said they let your actions go unpunished because of your grief," she encroached toward an argument.

I knew how she felt—trying so hard not to be helpless. I met her eyes wearily. I had tried too. I tried everything, and it was going to get her killed. The price of blasphemy was death, not just of the blasphemer, but of his whole line. Every soldier would die because of me unless I followed in my master's footsteps. It wouldn't save my captains, but it would save our men.

"I have no doubt that is what they told Xael," I said. Whatever they may have told the boy, no action went without consequence in this empire. Letting me live was temporary and only for the sake of completing my punishment.

"But Master San, you have no heir," she kept on.

"And I never will," I said, tone rising with my temper. Even if I did, they would kill the child too. Whether I had an heir or not, this was for the best. "They will be coming to make an example of the Dragon lineage. If you offer my head, it should be enough for our soldiers…maybe even you."

Severing my head would show they had forsaken me and carried out my punishment in full. I still doubted it would be enough for the emperor to spare my captains of imprisonment or execution, but a chance was better than none.

Her voice raised to match mine. "We are ready to die as part of this lineage."

I snapped, "I'm not!"

I wiped sweat from my burning forehead. "I'm not ready to answer for your lives like this. As an heir, I have failed to upkeep my master's name. As a master, I can still bear the responsibility of my soldiers' lives. I can answer for both with seppuku."

My master had said the only way to save our lineage was in an honorable death, but I had dug a hole so deep that only defiling my corpse could save them. I failed him then and now. I tried to talk him out of it, but this was how it was always going to end, and he knew that. I should have died with him, but I kept striving and it was for nothing…just like he said. If anyone was preeminent, it was him. I clenched my eyes, remembering his last moments. He had been so brave and so sad in those seconds. It was the way it had to be. So why did it haunt me still? Why did his blood weigh so heavily on my shoulders? I shook my head and the thoughts scattered. I couldn't think clearly with the pulsating ache in my head.

I made a mistake, my dream reverberated in my mind. I rubbed my temples, settling on my own two feet.

I made a mistake too. Many mistakes. Falling in line with the Snake, abandoning my master's teachings, focusing on a temporary solution—the list could go on. The Leopard did not deserve defamation any more than Master Hito had, and it was all for nothing.

Kirima wished for the empire to show me mercy, but I had spent long enough conquering countries to know Xinyue knew nothing of mercy. Master Hito was the only person left with both desire and power to offer compassion even to the conquered…even to me.

It's not too late for you, the dream-dragon rattled in my head.

Captain Chiyo set her lips in a tight line. She moved to retrieve her helmet and my wakizashi. As she did, I slipped into the training yard. To one side, a calm stone garden faced the open cliffside, overlooking miles of sharp blue mountainscape. To the other, a stone platform skirted with punching beams, rotating dummies, and other equipment faced the rocky path down to the barracks.

"I can finally speak freely, and you refuse to listen." Master Hito's voice came from the dragon that had moved into the center of my focus. It looked familiar—like the mockery of a memory.

"I've lost my sanity," I mumbled to myself, folding—or more like sloppily crumpling—onto my knees at the edge of the garden. A light pink radiated from the horizon meeting the dusky blue, like cherry blossoms on a bright spring day.

The expanse was as beautiful as the first day I saw it as a young boy. Master Hito brought me here right after the Festival of Heirs two decades ago. He taught me to meditate. Oh, how I had needed it. My life was upended, though it was in all of the best ways. I had a home, a people, a purpose, a passion, and a father. Everything I had lost to the empire, he gave back to me. And now I lost it all again, adding my sanity to the list.

"You've lost your way; there is a difference," the voice said, brushing against my shoulder. I shivered at how real it felt.

"My path is clear to me," I bristled. "As Master Hito's was to him."

"I am a poor example," it sighed.

"You are a figment of my imagination," I parried. I wanted him back so badly, my mind had made him into a monster.

The dragon quieted as Captain Chiyo approached from the rear, armor clattering with each step. I extended my hand for the sword. Reluctantly, she passed the blade into my calloused hands. She set two glasses of rice wine, ink, and paper in front of me.

So, this was the sanguine chagrin Master Hito had felt.

I stared at the paper until the sun was a complete, radiant circle over the furthest mountain peak. My death poem… Master Hito's tanka poem was perfect. It was sad, and yet had nothing to do with him. It was elegant and yet searing. As in everything, I would never match his proficiency. I hefted the brush and wiped the back of my hand across my burning forehead.

Illustrious sun,

reign indomitably true

like summer monsoons.

Indulge, O weeping mountains,

in indiscriminate light.

As I set the quill on the ground, I mused, "You disagree with my decision to commit seppuku. Does that reduce its sacrifice?"

The captain paused before replying, "It is a great sacrifice, but one you needn't make for us. We would follow you to any end, Dragon master."

The dragon slid around me to look at the paper. Its head rose even as its chest sank heavily. I warily watched it glide, worrying that if it became too real, I would lose myself to its odd realm.

"Do you resent it?" I asked, taking a deep breath. It did little to calm my beating heart or settle the churning in my head. "That this decision could have been yours to make?"

"Master Hito chose you for good reason. I could never envy what requires such forbearance," she said softer than I had ever heard her speak.

"Well, I won't tell if you don't," I said with a wry smile, handing her one of the shots meant to ease my suffering. "Please."

"I would be honored," she said, taking the glass and tapping it to mine. Only in this empire could two warriors from opposite lands share in a tradition not even our own. I wondered if I would miss this life or if I would remember it at all.

One swig for taste and one more for good measure. The glass tinked as I set it on the stone path. I enjoyed one last look at the mountains and drew my blade into a reverse grip. Captain Chiyo hovered behind me with her katana ready to sever my spine at the first sign of pain. My stomach preemptively moiled around my abdomen.

Only a week had passed since I stood in Captain Chiyo's position, agonizing over how I could change my master's mind. If only it had been as simple as refusing to take part, but his mind was set and I wouldn't let him die alone. Both then and now, all that I could do was the least that anyone could do.

So, I plunged my wakizashi into my gut.

A chill passed over the mountain as Kirima grunted and she struggled with the odd blade. She ripped the sword from my cold, weak hands. The dragon, an ever clearer hallucination, snarled at the intruder as Captain Chiyo stood in shock.

"What are you doing?" Kirima's shouts echoed in my ears. She had appeared just as the tip of the blade pierced my gut and seized it from my hands.

"Give it back!" I pleaded, uselessly reaching for my sword. My head was burning something wretched. "Why are you even here?"

"I was sent to scout before the assault," she said.

"Oh, thanks for interrupting so you can *really* complicate things!" I put a hand to my head. On the coldest days, when all the soldiers hunkered in their barracks, Master Hito would make me stand in a half-sitting stance while snow piled over my feet and the wind cut into my bones. My sweat would freeze as soon as it formed and ice would crystalize my eyelashes. Those memories were warmer than the chills seizing my muscles, and yet my forehead felt as if it might combust.

"Sh-should I attack?" Captain Chiyo asked, uncertainty hitching her voice.

"That depends," I said looking at Kirima, "Are you going to give back my wakizashi so I can finish the ritual?"

She threw it off the mountainside defiantly and spat, "I will not let you scorn Master Feiyu's kindness."

"You insufferable housecat! Your master sent me back to make a spectacle of the Dragon lineage's demise. *I* am trying to thwart that." The angrier I got, the less I could control the quivering.

She jutted a finger in my face. "That is not why he let you go."

"You just admitted you were scouting for an assault," I said, unsure who was in a greater state of confusion.

"That's true, but, well… I need to ask for your help," she added the last part in a quiet grumble. I made to stand, lightheadedness immediately overtaking me. The spectral dragon caught me just before Captain Chiyo helped me the rest of the way up. "What's wrong with you?" Kirima asked, her wrinkled visage softening.

"I can still feel your master's kindness," I grumbled sarcastically.

"He said you would recover quickly," she said lightly.

"It's my fault. I woke you too soon," the dragon said, mocking me with my master's voice. "We weren't done deliberating."

"Would you go away!" I shouted before I could think better of it. "I…"

I trailed off, not knowing how to explain to Kirima and Captain Chiyo I had gone mad. It was embarrassing enough to fail the ascension, but to lose my mind in the process was humiliating.

"That's why you're sick," Kirima realized. "Master Feiyu said he unlocked something in you. You haven't reconciled it, have you?"

"Unlocked? Like my chakra?" I fumbled with my elusive thoughts. They slunk away like the creeping feeling in my gut.

"I guess." She shrugged. "He said I wasn't ready to know."

I looked at the dragon, taking its existence seriously for the first time. In an unsettling way, it had the same look Master Hito always got when I realized he was right. I held a finger to the dragon, still doubting the reality of him. He smiled and rushed into me, rippling through me like the surface of a lake. I lurched, lethargy filling my joints.

"What can you tell me of the troops?" I asked Kirima weakly.

"Master Jai is leading two of his legions, advised by Shintaro," Kirima said, stepping forward to offer her hand. I took it and started a slow return to the warmth of my room.

"Shintaro wouldn't have sent you here to scout against me unless he gave you false information," I said.

"He is confident he has twisted the right weakness," she said with a shudder.

"And that is?"

"They have Master Feiyu in the dungeon." Her eyes chilled like the northern wind.

"The dungeon? On what authority? What charge?"

"On authority of the emperor for treason," she said. Her whole body slouched as she chose her next words. "This is supposed to free him, but I know it won't. Master Feiyu listened to you, and so he sought answers and stumbled onto troubling findings."

"That the emperor hired foreigners?" I figured.

"No, that the lineage of the Vermillion has taken the emperor hostage and is forcing him to play his part while the Vermillion is reinstated," she said. Captain Chiyo, the dragon, and I all froze in shocked silence. The Vermillion died in an earth-shattering battle to carve Xinyue's place in the East eras ago. It wasn't possible for them to be at fault here. Then again, if I could breathe fire, who was I to speak of the impossible. "Master Feiyu talked to Master Kashvi, and soon after, Emperor Xinya claimed you and he devised an elaborate plan to overthrow the empire."

"That's ridiculous!" I seethed.

"Quite, but no one questions the emperor." Her gaze softened on me, an apology resting on her lips.

Shivers ran up my spine as Captain Chiyo opened the door into my room. Inside, the sound of the wind whipped against the sturdy walls. For all of the comfort this room provided, my men were still in danger and my lineage in ruins. Kirima now found herself in the same position I had just a few weeks ago, trying to save my master and his lineage.

"You want me to help you break him out?" I guessed.

"No, the tunnels are crawling with snakes. I want you to help me free the emperor," she said.

"Oh, yes, that will be so much easier." My words dripped sarcasm. "Besides, I would rather die than help that coward."

"If you help us, I am sure the emperor will restore Master Hito's name," she said. I paused at that. I could make that demand. The emperor had already proven himself too cowardly to refuse in the face of those more powerful than he. What a pathetic excuse of a leader.

"Let's say I successfully rebuff Jai's assault with my half-legion…" I said, settling onto my bedroll. "When did you say they would be here?"

"At the current speed, four days." She knelt by me.

"Say I rebuff them in four days, what is your plan to exorcize the ghosts?" I asked.

"I don't know," she admitted.

Kirima dipped her head, her hair quickly covering her pooling tears. I gaped at her, at a loss as to what I did. Her shoulders shuddered as her fists clenched her clothes. Silent tears dripped onto the cotton draped over her knees. I put an apprehensive hand on her shoulder, unsure how to help. She collapsed into me, arms pulling against my back.

My face flushed as I caught Captain Chiyo watching smugly. She gestured outside, bowed, and slipped out the door. I breathed, thankful for the privacy.

Kirima's sobs tortured my heart but all the agony in the world couldn't have alleviated her worries. I pulled a little tighter. She coerced her tears to subside to sniffles. Her hands brushed the streaks of water off my back shakily.

"I'll think of something," I promised, carefully covering my doubts.

"I never thought… You must think I'm pretty pathetic," she said wringing her hands.

I paused for too long, my thoughts moving like molasses. Her face turned tomato red and I rushed to say something, anything.

"No, no," I finally spit. "I, uh, think you'll make a powerful leader."

"You don't have to lie to make me feel better," she grumbled.

I managed a lopsided yet heartfelt smile. "I once followed a man with as big of a heart as yours."

"Everyone knows Master Hito was a stern master." She chuckled, wiping a stray streak of water.

"Yes, you have that going for you too." I laughed and winced at the curdling in my stomach. "Now, maybe if you tell them my full legion has already returned it will buy us a fifth day. Will they see anyone leaving the mountain?"

She nodded. "Scouts are positioned at the base to keep information from coming and going. They have legions marching on the Dragon's other fortresses as we speak so a complete victory is required here."

"Shintaro is strategic, if nothing else," I admitted. "How did you get in?"

"I came from the cliff," she said.

"Oh, now everyone can climb five kilometers of sheer rock with mountain vipers in every crevasse, huh?" I puffed. One boy does it and suddenly it's so feasible.

"Don't be dramatic, just those trained for it," she said. "Do you not have any among you who can scale it?"

"Xael can…but I'm told he is still recovering from carrying me up," I said.

"That boy carried you up the mountainside?" Her eyes bulged.

"He's impressive. But even if he could get down, he wouldn't make it to the next fortress in time…"

"I'll leave my horse," she said. "It may not be a guarantee, but if you can get a man down, you can warn your other men. None of the other masters or heirs have been sent to those. The captains are anticipating an easy reception into the camps before turning on them."

"Won't it be suspicious if you return without one?"

"I will tell them you had guards watching the cliff, so I had to leave the horse or be spotted," she answered.

"Guards on the cliff seem a decent idea after this week," I said with an eye roll.

Kirima leaned in and tossed her arms around me. A quiet gratitude passed between us before she let go and traded with Captain Chiyo. I struggled to make a strategy in my hazy state, but I had a few ideas. I needed to talk to my soldiers.

"Master San, you need rest," Captain Chiyo said, voice echoing in her helmet.

"I need to talk to them first," I said. I gripped her forearm and hoisted myself to my feet.

Lightheadedness immediately stole my balance and my vision. The world went black before I even hit the ground.

21

As I stood above Master Hito in this familiar dream, I picked apart the phenomenon. The air was completely still. This time, I had full control over myself, as did the dragon I took to be Master Hito. In a cathartic moment, I threw my sword to the ground and snatched his wrists with claws of my own.

"You cannot change what has been," it rasped with closed eyes.

"Why are you haunting me? Are you a chakra point?"

He breathed a laugh and wagged his head. "When a master passes on, their heir takes that place and begins searching for an inheritor."

"Yes," I said, "I know the cycle."

"Oh, do you?" it asked, pulling from my grip easily and drilling yellow serpent eyes into mine. Fear washed over me as the creature straightened, several heads higher than mine. "Then you ought to know the answer to your question."

I filtered through what I knew and how it might relate to whatever Master Feiyu had let loose inside of me. I resented whatever he had done to me. Facing my master as a monster was something the Snakes would inflict if they knew how. Although, this dragon was more a person than a monster.

"You are the piece of Master Hito that remains in me?" I postulated, intonation rising at the end.

"Close. I am the essence of Master Hito," he explained. "A master is never beyond teaching and an attentive student never beyond saving."

The essence of him? Was it my memory of who he was at his core? I looked at the dragon. He didn't carry any human characteristics anymore. Master Hito was a terror to behold and altogether separate from me. I was always striving to emulate him and never quite succeeding. Could it really be him?

"I don't understand," I fumbled. "I can't understand."

"Until you pass on, watching over you is my charge," he said. "This is my last chance to guide and exhort you."

"You've been watching this whole time?" I asked, a stab of betrayal blindsiding me. I failed him. How could I feel as if he abandoned me?

"I've been trying to reach you, but you were so determined to do this alone that I couldn't get through your thick skull," Master Hito chided.

"I wanted to make it right," I said, kneeling in front of him as I had done so many times before. "I wanted to bring rightful praise to your name."

"San, you are not an heir that must live up to his father and lord—you are my scion, chosen because you have already lived up to my expectations. I am so proud to call you mine."

Tears stung my eyes.

"But I haven't… I endangered your friend, discredited your ally, and may have destroyed your legacy." I was the worst heir in the history of lineages.

"You acted with more dignity as my scion than I did as your master. You have done well," he breathed, placing a clawed hand over my shoulder. "But you have forgotten the first and most important thing I ever taught you."

As a child in the shadow of his father, I raised my eyes in grief and awe. I was sure I had lost him. He died—I severed his spine myself after his blade crossed his abdomen. Guilt pulled at my heart as relief welled in my eyes. I waded through my emotions searching for the first lesson. He had taught me a form before I was even one of his. Every form began and ended with the same movement.

"Bowing to something beyond ourselves—to the Giver of Strength."

He nodded. "Our esteem is of little importance to him, but the way in which we use his gifts matters greatly."

I blinked, processing his words and their meaning. He talked about this force as if it were a real man.

"I lost sight of this and nearly led you to the same downfall," he said. "Please forgive me, San."

I rose into him, clutching his scaled forearm and throwing my other arm around him with a solid thump. I wasn't sure if I believed in this Giver of Strength, but I would follow any path my master walked. I had to restore his name now that I knew he resided with me. The empire had to accept him as the greatest master to ever live.

I had so many more questions to ask, but they would have to wait. "I feel our time is running out."

The dragon let out a breath of smoke in agreement.

"Will you grant me your qi to lead our men to victory?"

The dragon puffed a steaming breath, "The Dragon qi belongs to you as much as it ever did to me. May we accomplish a bloodless conquest."

My senses returned to the world as it was. I rose to my feet, this time with ease. My fever had broken in the night and the birds' lighthearted melody danced from the windowsill. I caught movement to my side and found the dragon filling the room. With a shared nod, we descended into the camp.

"The master!" A soldier hollered to his comrades.

Soldiers brushed off their dark uniforms and pulled their hands into formal salutes. Their eyes sparked with life as one by one they saw me entering the camp. Where I expected fear and resentment, I found respect and relief. Chills ran up my spine as pride filled my chest. These were my men—hopeful in the face of tumultuous times.

"Master San, your timing is impeccable," Captain Chiyo said, as she ducked under one of the barrack tent flaps. Her eyes glimmered behind her monstrous faceplate. "You look well."

"Better than ever," I agreed. "How goes the preparations?"

"We have added fortifications where they won't be noticed, begun rationing, and have gathered many barrels of water," she said. "The men have worked hard and are committed to training the newer troops after hours."

"Speaking of newer troops," I said, continuing my patrol through the large fortification. "How is Xael?"

She walked for a silent moment. "No signs of waking… Would you like to see him?"

I nodded. I would need to rally the soldiers soon, but my plan required Xael's expertise. He rested beyond the dusty-brown flaps of a largely empty medical tent. A few soldiers tended to minor injuries acquired from rushing to prepare the camp. Xael was the only immobile patient, lying like the dead. His qi wrapped around every inch of him like bandages.

He still wore the same uniform he had worn during my fight with the Leopard. It was tattered and torn all over the place. His hands were healed, and the newly closed puncture wounds covering his arms and legs slowly receded. I reached my hand to touch his sweat-slicked forehead, but the energy surrounding him stung my finger like a scorpion.

"It's like he's burning," Captain Chiyo said, "No one can touch him."

I looked to my master and extended my hand. He shrugged

his hulking shoulders and engulfed my hand with translucent, sea-foam claws. I pressed in again. The dragon cringed at the painful prickling but pressed into it. The wrapping unraveled around Xael like a rope tossed over a cliff. Fear gripped my heart. I needed him but as more wrappings fell away, I realized how exposed it left him.

Xael snapped awake with a choked cry.

"You're ok, Xael," I said, hand on his shoulder. "You've done well."

"S—" His eyes flashed to my hand. "Master San, you've awakened."

A lopsided smile found its way on my face. He was learning to use double meanings. "Yes, and I have a brave young warrior to thank for it. How are you?"

Color painted his face as his qi returned to a flowing pattern around him. "I feel like I slept for days."

"It seems we both did. Would you deliberate over a meal with us? A great battle is coming and we have little time." I asked with a gesture to Captain Chiyo.

Xael looked around for someone I might be talking to. Finding the tent behind him empty, he pointed a finger at himself with eyes the size of plates.

"Oh, I— Of course, yes!"

"But first, I have a few questions, one inheritor to another," I said, earning a brow raise from Captain Chiyo. I turned to her. "We will meet you in the war room."

Captain Chiyo bowed and made her leave, patting Xael firmly

on the shoulder as she went. Xael straightened and flashed a grin. She always knew how to speak to our men.

I helped Xael off of the sick bed cautiously. He bounced from one foot to the other as if testing out a new set of legs. A smile grew past his cheeks, lifting his ears. While Chiyo went right, I pulled Xael to the left, down a secluded path that skirted the outside of the fortress. The hardy trees were a stone's throw away, but their branches often blew onto the path, making it less useful for training runs than laps around the barracks.

"Did you rest well?" I asked.

"Yes, Master San."

"We're friends, Xael. 'San' is fine." His smile dipped ever so slightly as his eyes stuck to mine. He nodded. It was time I understood what those eyes hid. "Thank you for bringing me home."

"You're not angry? I broke our deal…"

"I was, at first," I admitted. "But then Captain Chiyo told me about a boy that had no friends or stake here, and sacrificed for me and my home anyway. A real hero."

Xael blushed a new shade of red and tripped over a vine. I caught him by the forearms before he hit the ground and hoisted him back to his feet.

"I don't understand you, Xael. Why did you do it?"

"What does it matter?" he asked with a shrug. "I did what I did and I'd do it again."

"I sacrificed everything to save my lineage. I laid down my life for it and I would have done far more—I still will. But you have your own lineage. You should be off finding an heir and building your numbers." Why would anyone sacrifice their lineage for another? That is what I could not understand.

Xael grabbed a stick along the path and started whacking spindly shoots as we passed. We followed the trail quietly as he sighed and huffed to himself. His qi swam around him like a human-sized hurricane and his smile had long since faded. Xael finally tossed the stick further into the wooded side of the path.

"I just wanted to impress someone," he said. "Prove I was an equal."

"Impress your former master?" I guessed, although I already knew I was right by the desperation I had first seen in his eyes. Knowing Master Hito was watching changed everything for me. It wasn't a death wish for his lineage to be secured now, it was a living wish that only I could grant. Xael had to feel the same, trying to prove himself to someone far greater than himself.

Xael nodded gently. "He—well—I never learned the combative side of the Binturong lineage. When I saw you fight..." he trailed off. "I'll never be like that."

I clapped his shoulder. "You're a fine heir. Your master must be proud, and if you're willing and we all survive this, I'd be honored to teach you a thing or two about fighting."

Xael beamed. "You'll teach me to fight?!"

"Yes, well," I sighed, "I hate to say it, but I have another favor to ask first..."

22

"Sssan, you decided to join the parlay." Shintaro's sibilant voice vexed my ears. It seemed Kirima was unable to stall their progress, but knowing Shintaro, he had purposefully marched faster after she left in case she was captured.

We had agreed on a meeting place halfway up the mountain. It was an open plateau on the fastest of the two ascents. Most of the passage was jagged and narrow, with slick vines and moss creeping on either side, but these plateaus became more common closer to the base of the Serpent's Teeth. Here, my soldiers could watch from the next ridge, and Jai's were in arrow range at the opposite edge.

Jai stood with his chest puffed out in a rugged, pewter-colored uniform just beyond the range of my flames. His qi covered his center in a thick mass that extended over the bō staff he proudly held between us. Shintaro's qi flitted about him, chaotic and unrefined. It must have been so obvious to the masters I was not ready to face them.

Master Hito warned me the day would come when I would be at the disadvantage in parlay, but how could I have anticipated this? The empire itself was standing against its oldest lineage. I rested my hand on the hilt of my katana, and took a deep breath.

"I believe my parlay is with Master Jai," I said, watching Shintaro with the corner of my eye.

"You brought your second; I brought mine," said Jai.

"The Snake, really?" I goaded his ego. "You must care little for your men."

"Says the outnumbered general."

"I guess I should say you don't believe in your men then, bringing two legions to meet my one."

"Shintaro warned me you would do this," Jai said. "I came to clear the air, that is all."

"Then clear away." I crossed my arms.

The air was thick, as the sun blistered in the clearing. Nothing dared disturb the tense silence, save for the distant rumbling of a waterfall. I knew Jai would demand my surrender, but the cost of surrender would be too high.

"This mountain is mine in the name of the emperor. You are trespassers."

I coughed out a laugh. "The Rhino is the new protector of the inner fortifications?" What had our empire come to, putting the Rhino in charge of *my* fortresses?

"What's funny, Dragon?"

"You break fortresses, Jai, not maintain them. This is ridiculous," I said.

"Massster Jai," Shintaro corrected as if he cared. I rolled my eyes.

Jai was many things—proud, brave, stalwart, and even noble in all of the best ways—but he was not a sentry. Of all the lineages, the Rhino was the one most affected by the lack of war. Even the Snake had a job in the lull as warden of the imperial prisons, but the Rhino just waited for the next offensive. We had speculated a war was coming on the pagoda rooftop, but not against each other. Heaviness clutched my chest for the alliance—even friendship—we once shared.

"If you don't yield, I will lay siege," Jai warned, thumping his bō staff on the ground.

"Siege, really?" I laughed. "You must have all the time in the world."

"Master San, I have ten thousand men and you have four thousand. Yield."

"You cannot win." Shintaro's words dripped with conceit.

I huffed and turned to Captain Chiyo. "If we surrender, our men go to the gallows or the dungeons…if they make it that far."

She tensely glanced to the men on the ridge.

"It would be better to starve," she agreed.

"I will not yield," I shouted. "You come to my mountain under the orders of a coward and ask me to surrender my men to imprisonment or execution. If you expected me to agree, you have both gone mad."

"What if all we required was your head? They could go free at the cost of one life," Shintaro bartered.

"No," I said as surely as ever. The time for abandoning them had passed. I would stand with my men, and we would face the future together. Master Hito's azure qi swirled around me, filling my veins with vigor. "But I would accept a duel of generals."

Shintaro grabbed Jai before he could issue the challenge. They had a whispered discourse before turning back to the parlay. I knew Jai wanted to fight me more than anything, just as I wanted to fight him. Using troops was necessary, but we were both raised on the belief that what can be settled among masters should be settled among masters.

"No challenge," Jai ground out. He looked to Captain Chiyo and bellowed for the men on the ridge to hear, "If you bring his head, the siege will end."

My eyes widened in surprise. I could have predicted such underhanded tactics from Shintaro, but it went against everything Jai stood for to try turning my own men against me. There was a time Jai counted among my few friends but this…he would have to hate me a great deal to try to turn my fortress into a pit of vipers.

At a clear impasse, we parted ways. We met our archers on the ridge and began the trek back to the fort. Captain Chiyo boiled beneath her armor at Jai's brazen proffer.

"If any of you even think about that Snake's suggestion, I will have your skins," she seethed.

The most senior of them replied, "If you think us traitors, gut us where we stand."

"No need for that," I said, pulling ahead of them. "No one called for my abdication before today, I doubt they will now."

"Men are guided by their stomachs; time will tell their loyalty," she said, mistrust brewing in her.

"Then have faith. They were trained by a woman," I countered with a grin.

Since we left the parlay, I felt a prickle at the back of my neck. But every time I turned, no one was there. There were enough trees and boulders to hide anyone skilled at remaining unseen and I already knew the emperor had sent an assassin once.

Twice, if you include Shintaro, given his lineage's history with assassination. I could be fairly certain Shintaro wouldn't challenge me himself, but who knew how many he might send for my head. I shook away the lurking feeling and kept my head on a swivel.

The camp jittered with anticipation, every eye tracking as we returned. Soldiers sat to the side, cleaning and sharpening their blades incessantly between tasks. Captain Chiyo moved from group to group, ensuring everything was being done with the utmost care. She shared in their worries and their work equally.

Their anxieties were well founded, though my only fear was that our victory would come through heavy bloodshed. Shintaro might have had ill intent, but the Rhino was a true lineage. Jai and his men were convinced this was right, and that frightened me most. Jai might decide this was a hill on which he and all of our men would die.

As I sat around one of the fires with a younger assortment, I asked, "How many of you have heard the tale of the coliseum conquest?"

I would be a fool to ignore Captain Chiyo's concerns. For all the time I spent training with Master Hito, she had spent more among our soldiers. I believed their spirits were their driving force, not their gut, but if she was right, this would be a strenuous trial for them. I could not add to their rations, but I could add to their hearts through story as Master Hito had done for me so many times.

I must have told a dozen stories before the fires burned low and a figure caught the corner of my eye. Soldiers bowed and headed for their beds as I returned to the peak, carefully checking my blind spots. The hairs on the back of my neck stood electrified. I was being watched.

I left the door to my home open and started a fire for tea. I placed two cups on the small table and knelt on the purpleheart floor with a view of the door, hands ready to strike. The figure would have to appear sooner or later, and I hoped they would choose a conversation over their death.

In the late evening, the black walnut walls looked almost as dark as a moonless night. On most nights, it would be a nice ambience with the flickering lanterns hung along the walls, but this night, the shadows seemed to crawl. As the teapot began to whistle, a chill snaked up my back.

"Expecting me?" Kirima's quiet whisper asked as she appeared off in a corner, out of the door's view.

I stood and closed the door. "I wasn't sure if it was you or an assassin, but I thought tea might be inviting either way."

Her laugh came and went like a vapor in the wind. "Shintaro is pressuring for that, but I doubt he will win Jai over on it."

"I will keep an eye out nonetheless." A long silence passed as I poured two cups of jasmine tea and passed one to her. Her hands cradled the teacup like a newly hatched chick. I had questions, but I feared saying too much. "Did you come up the cliff again?"

"No, I followed you from the parlay." She had remained unnoticed for that long? I knew I was being watched, but I had no idea the extent of her abilities. "Shintaro and Jai believe you have some trick up your sleeve… You do, don't you?"

I sighed and took a sip. "The less you know, the better, Kirima. Just focus on making Shintaro believe you're upset about your master and being compliant for his sake."

"But I have to know, San. Please…" The desperation in her eyes stirred up everything I felt as I pleaded with Master Hito to find another way that kept us together. The soul-rending pain of separation had harrowed me for weeks leading up to Master Hito's death and it nearly broke me. I couldn't watch Kirima suffer the same.

"Were you listening to my stories?" I asked. She nodded slowly. "It's seldom obvious, but there's always another way, even if you have to carve out the path yourself. Trust me, Kirima. I won't let you down."

Her lip quivered and her eyes closed. She nodded and set her tea on the table. "Thank you, San."

Kirima disappeared. One of my windows flapped open, the only sign of her vanishing. The truth was, if we won this exchange, it would be a dark horse victory. I could only hope her faith in me was well placed.

Under my breath, I muttered, "May we all find strength in the days to come."

By the end of the second week, an uneasiness had fallen over the camp like a damp blanket. The soldiers grew more restless and a few quarrels had sparked among them, although Captain Chiyo's stern warnings startled them back in line for the time being. I caught several eyes idly watching the last barrels of food dwindle.

"They grow tired of waiting," Master Hito commented from our peak.

I sighed heavily. "I suppose it is time to act."

"You have kindled their hearts well, but even the brightest fire will burn out without fuel."

I hoped Kirima's heart had remained alight. If she could wait just a little longer, I would free her from the Snake's service. "It must be excruciating to work alongside such a sadistic sleaze."

"The Snake earned its spot among us," Master Hito said. "Although I will not be surprised when it earns its execution either."

I signaled to Captain Chiyo, and she gathered two thousand of our soldiers beneath the peak and stationed several runners among the mass of men and women.

I proclaimed from my perch, "Soldiers of the Dragon lineage, your strength is legendary and your hearts true. We have fought many battles together but none as important as this, when the empire has been taken captive by those who hold no claim to the throne. Today, we fight for our families! We fight for the truth! We fight for a legacy that will not die quietly!"

A cheer erupted from the soldiers, carrying itself on the wind.

"Eat a full meal and prepare yourselves for victory. We descend when the sun reaches its peak."

I led the march down the mountain as thundering footsteps followed. Even coming from the high ground, two thousand men stood little chance against ten thousand. If I miscalculated, the ground would be flooded with the blood of many brave warriors. I stole a glance to my nearest unit. Would they be the first to fall? Would their screams fill my ears? Would it all be on my shoulders?

Every question weighed heavier on my heart than the one before. I only inherited this position a few weeks ago and I thought I could win a battle against two of the rhino's best legions? I looked to the units even further back. Would my arrogance cost their lives?

We were only halfway down the mountain and just starting to spread out at points, taking slightly different descents. I could turn everyone back to the fortress right now.

I slipped on a clump of moss and narrowly caught myself on the next tree.

"Breathe easy, Master San." Master Hito drifted beside me, floating down steeper sections.

"Easy for you to say. We just join you if I'm wrong."

He moved in front of me, standing on his back legs. His stature loomed over me. I hunkered down and held my hand in the air, signaling the troops to hold their march. Whispers passed along the message.

"You are the dragon master; act like it," Master Hito breathed menacingly. "You have been given great power. Do not let your fear cloud your vision."

I straightened, remembering what he taught me. I was trained for this—to serve my soldiers faithfully and use my gifts to the best of my ability. Overpowering the Rhino was the easiest portion of my plan. If I let my grit falter here, I would never reach the throne to free the emperor and make my demands of him.

I strode through Master Hito's ethereal form, catching the first glint of a scout's horn several meters away. I ducked behind a tree and pointed out the scout to the closest unit. An arrow thudded into the tree just beside the Rhino soldier, startling him right into the arms of the soldier who snuck up behind him.

We left the man bound to the tree and gagged. The next half of the ruck would be a grueling march as we watched for horn bearers. Surprise was an ally we could not afford to lose.

Every cracking stick and rustling leaf earned a silencing shush from fellow comrades. Their anticipation grew with each step closer to the battlefield. The moon's rise only served to worsen the condition. Steep, rough hills hid squads from each other and offset our lines. The legions of tall, winding trees with stark white bark did little to restrain the wind as it grew to a howl, cutting a chill into our bones. Our progress slowed to a crawl through the final stretch.

Finally, with the moon high, we reached the final line of trees before the bottom plateau.

"Ready your torches," I whispered to the two closest units, "but wait to light them."

They passed the instructions on to the units closest to them and every man armed himself with two torches.

Jai had made camp with just enough space that we would have to meet his troops on flat ground. Even worse, we would have to cross the gap to them in open fields, taking heavy casualties. I looked to the Rhino's endless rows of tents, changing the skyline. All I could do was wait and hope everything went to plan.

Seconds turned to minutes and minutes turned to hours. The moon was well into its descent when I saw a flash to my right. One of the men tried to spark his torch and three others struggled with him. I snatched the flint from the man and pulled him to his feet.

"Trust me. The time is near."

As I turned my eyes back to the field, whispers carried like wind around me. Without instruction, my words passed to each soldier in the militia. I leaned against the tree, watching the moon continue its fall from the sky. As the voices hushed, the horizon ignited with brilliant light. Chills washed over my skin as thousands of lights engulfed the far side of the plateau. Men rose from the tall grass with torches and katanas in hand, ready to attack with a single call.

Xael did it. He saved me again.

"Light the torches!" I shouted.

Before the words finished leaving my mouth, two thousand sparks flashed among the trees, lighting one torch, and spreading to the next. A roar filled the air from beyond the camp and we rejoined with a battle cry from the depths of our souls.

I breached the tree line, shrouded by the Dragon's qi, and bellowed, "You are surrounded by legions. Yield!"

23

"Yield!" I shouted to the encampment of warriors with a voice that shook the ground.

Jai ran from his tent to see the lights on both sides flickering against my armored warriors.

Don't look too hard, I silently prayed.

More torches lit to either side of the camp, surprising even me. Row upon row of monstrous masks with barbed teeth bobbed above the tall grass. Xael had found a way to send even more reinforcements.

Xael entrusted his life to me, and I to him. If Xael wasn't already an inheritor, I would claim him as my own. Envy crept into my thoughts. Did his master value him like I did?

Seeing the peril, Jai hastened to shout, "Duel! Winner takes, with no bloodshed!"

I couldn't help but smile, giving an affirming nod to the

squad at my side. Everything had gone perfectly—just as I had planned it.

"I accept your challenge."

I unsheathed my katana and swept a clean circle through the tall grass several times, clearing an oval section for the dueling ground. Four of Jai's warriors brought large torches and pounded them into the ground around the circle.

"To the yield?" I asked.

"Or death," Jai responded.

Shintaro slipped out of a tent and slunk to the other side of the ring. Captain Chiyo stepped to take my katana when Kirima appeared, a fire in her eyes.

"Stay with your men," she said to the captain. "I will watch here."

I nodded to Captain Chiyo, who dutifully strapped my katana to herself and receded. When I won, I needed her there to hold my men back from a needless assault. The Dragon shrouded my entire body with intense qi. My hand sharpened into claws and my skin strengthened like the bronze it emulated.

"I knew your loyalties would quickly waver," Shintaro hissed. "Even with your master one word from death, you ssside with a traitor."

"We will get it all back," Kirima bit out. "And when we do, your lineage will crumble."

Though I could not see the former Rhino master, I felt his presence with Jai.

Jai stood like a mountain before me with every intent to kill. That dagger look hadn't left his eyes since the parade. Qi sharpened around Jai's hands, feet, knees, elbows, and head like horns—all major breaking and striking points.

"Can your defense hold against the fortress breaker?" Kirima asked.

"Jai will provide his own defeat," I said.

Chest full of pride and heart full of ambitions, I stepped to the center. Jai met me halfway. We shared a bow, and I remembered my training.

May my gifts grant a complete victory, I silently prayed.

"Begin," Shintaro said.

Jai charged with a furious battle cry. He startled me sideways with a stomp at my closest foot. I narrowly bent beneath a rippling hook and swiped a claw at his leg. An elbow landed squarely into my back—the price for lingering—slamming me into the grass. Pain seared to the base of my skull. Jai had grown quickly into his newfound power.

Another stomp plummeted toward me just like the first night of the festival, only this time he intended to crush my head. I rolled to the side, missing a series of stomps until my hands vaulted me to my feet.

Heavy breaths puffed from my chest, carrying smoke with them. I dodged another swing and caught Kirima's horrified expression in my periphery. Shintaro threw a bō staff into Jai's hands.

"No one sssaid anything about weapon hindrances," he snickered.

Kirima had no sword to offer as her lineage trained for distance and Captain Chiyo was a length away.

"Anyone who needs a weapon to succeed has no right to the victory," my master reminded me.

I jumped over the deep purple bō Jai swung at me, and caught a heel kick to the ribs that flung me to the edge of the circle. I cringed with a hand over the bruising. Hand to bō …

What do I do? I thought desperately. Every man in my army had done exactly as I asked no matter how difficult and now everything relied on me.

"Wood burns," Master Hito's voice echoed in my head.

I opened my hands to the sky and let out a blaze of fire that should have turned them to ash. As Jai jabbed at my chest, I pivoted and grabbed the wooden weapon. It charred but didn't break. He ripped it back and swiped it at my injury.

In a moment of pure confidence, I stood my ground and sent a burning knife hand at the char point. It snapped just above his second hand. I snatched the broken wood from the air and flung it back at Jai. This was my chance. I channeled my qi into my fist and surged toward Jai. He dodged the wood, landing squarely into my dragon fist.

Jai dropped to the ground, chest rising and falling unsteadily. Master Rohak's qi blanketed Jai with protection though it would have done little to thwart me if I intended to kill the new master in this unconscious state.

With a fist raised, I yelled, "Victory!" My men reprised in glorious chant.

I turned to Shintaro, but he was already gone, slithering away in the grass like the coward he was. Kirima darted after him and snatched him above the tall grass by the scruff of his uniform.

"Time for our own duel," she snapped.

"To the death?" he asked with a sinister gleam.

"Kiri—"

She didn't let me finish. "I accept."

No one moved as the two heirs took to the center. I raked my hand through my hair, helplessness eating me alive. Kirima wafted qi, all too ready to begin. Shintaro cackled in his place, floating two flat hands in front of him like coiled cobras.

"Begin." The word tried to catch in my throat.

Shintaro's wide, forward-leaning stance screamed confidence as Kirima advanced cautiously. They circled each other slowly. Shintaro struck first with unbelievable speed. He shot his hand like lightning into her shoulder and quickly dipped beneath her swiping paw, shooting a devastating hand into her armpit.

I waited for her to fall, but she stood defiantly against another set of strikes. Her snarl deepened with every undefended blow.

"The leopard's conditioning is stunning, isn't it?" Master Hito commented beside me.

He's pulling his punches, I noted internally.

"Even so, anyone else would have succumbed by now."

Though she failed to land a single strike, Shintaro retreated. He was toying with her, like a mouse in an open field. Kirima panted sharp, quick breaths. The blows were not without cost. As Shintaro flashed a crooked grin at me, I realized Kirima was not the one being tormented. If he could not win the battle, he would make sure it was a pyrrhic victory for me.

"Isn't there anything we can do?" I asked my master under my breath.

A weight of silence fell as Shintaro snapped into action. He advanced with death in his movements. Kirima fell for his feinted jab at her throat bobbing off balance. His off hand snaked around her leg. She yelped as he toppled her and slammed her into the ground in an instant. My heart jumped to my throat. His hand shriveled back to three pronged fingers, going for the kill.

His fingers struck the ground where she laid just after her body vanished. Kirima appeared just to the side, sweeping Shintaro's knees to the ground. Another spinning kick narrowly missed his head as he flung himself to his feet. Kirima jutted toward him, fire in her eyes. Seeing her crashing elbow, he snapped to the side. He sent a knife hand at the back of her neck.

My heart skipped a beat when as I saw it. Kirima twirled with his oncoming hand, wrapping and throwing him like a swirling tornado. His gasp was met with immediate silence as she finished him with one leopard's fists to the temple. A nearly bloodless victory.

I tilted my head back, looking toward the stars and breathing, soaking in the relief. I understood her anger and desperation, but if she had died…I didn't know what I would have done. Wind whipped my hair across my face, bringing me back to the moment.

Captain Chiyo met with the other captains while their soldiers systematically disarmed the Rhino legions. Xael came running with a contagious smile.

"We did it!" he yelled.

I clapped his shoulder, jarring him off balance. "You brought more than I asked."

He took a deep breath and in one long-winded explanation said, "When I explained everything, Captain Jiro said the Rhino could have the fortress when they arrived. Someone needed to guard the perimeter and you would need the forces to take the capital. He sent his fastest horses to the other fortresses and several of them sent extra soldiers. Some were still filtering in when we lit the torches, but we couldn't wait any longer."

"Whoa, slow down," I said.

"Oh sorry, Master San. I've just been sitting in the grass for hours. It felt like *forever*."

"It was a long wait," I agreed. "Why don't you go blow off some steam carrying weapons from the camp?"

He nodded and darted after a group of soldiers.

"An impressive debut, Dragon master," Kirima said, throwing Shintaro over her shoulder. His qi drifted off him like the smoke of an extinguished flame.

"And to you as well. Shintaro's speed was only rivaled by your master's before today, although we could have used his information."

"I didn't kill him," she stated coolly. "He's just selfish enough to trade his life for information—otherwise I would have."

"Then we ought to tie them both to a post and get what we need quickly," I said.

Kirima secured manacles around Jai's hands and feet on the other side of the camp's banner pole. Shintaro was too squirmy for large metal clamps, so I cinched the ropes around him until I felt the bones in his wrists compress and grind into each other. I did every binding with the same amount of care and caution. He would not slip free on my watch.

A bucket of water jolted them both awake. Jai's sudden thrash knocked an elbow painfully into Shintaro's back. He writhed his head back into Jai's.

"Maybe we can leave them to interrogate each other." I chuckled to Kirima.

"Hilariousss." Shintaro sizzled in place, heat rising up his neck.

She clicked her teeth, "This isn't a time for jokes."

"I told you we needed more," Jai barked at his strategist.

"I told you we should have assassinated him in his camp," the Snake hissed.

Jai shook his head. "Dirty tactics."

"Alright." I had heard enough of their bickering. I still had a pledge to uphold and I would not be delayed again. With the way the clouds were clustering, a monsoon was nearing. "How much does Jai know?"

"About what?" the Rhino master asked.

"Yess, about what, Dragon massster?"

I warned bitterly, "Kirima is one straw from breaking your neck, Snake."

"We die with dignity," Jai said.

"You heard my orders," Shintaro snarked. He was miscalculating her ferocity. Her soft art could easily be mistaken for gentleness. It was deceptive in that way. Kirima was not gentle, she was disciplined, and he should have feared that discipline most of all.

Kirima snatched Shintaro by the hair and said, "Very well, you first."

Her hand coiled by her face.

"Wait," he blurted, "My release for information."

Predictable.

"Your life," Kirima bartered. "For *accurate* information."

"Because you would obviousssly be able to tell the difference," he hissed sarcastically, fidgeting his shoulders uncomfortably.

I knelt, my face in his, drilling my qi into him as I had done to Xael at the pagoda. He needed to feel how close to death he was. "If we die, so do you."

"You will die regardlesss."

"Then you would do well to think up *very* helpful information," Kirima said, releasing her grip.

"Coward," Jai spat. "This is not in the codes of war."

"Listen quietly. I don't want to gag you," I said. When all was said and done, Jai might apologize for all the trouble he caused.

"I will be ussseful."

"Who knows about the Vermillion?" I asked.

"No one," Shintaro said. I rested the tip of my katana on his thigh. His eyes narrowed into slits as the blade drew a bead of blood. It pressed a hiss from his lips, and I savored the discomfort he now endured.

"It's true, the Vermillion is dead," he alleged, struggling uselessly against his restraints. "These people called themselves the Vermillion and convinced the emperor they were ghosts having a rightful place among the lineages."

"Why attack the Dragon?" I pressed.

"Because the Dragon doesn't lisssten well." I sunk the katana deeper for the smarmy response. He was lying through his teeth. Shintaro always sought to look more knowledgeable and impressive than he really was. He winced and ground out, "Do you wish to sssay you do listen well, Dragon massster?"

"Do you claim to listen well?"

"Clearly better than you," he said with a grimace, shifting.

"So what? When we stood our ground, the emperor ordered an attack on all the lineages?" That sounded fictitious. I pulled my sword free and slowly cleaned the end of the blade on the collar of his grass-green uniform.

"When you joined the contest of heirs, the foreign master sent her most skilled heir to kill you, but who was to know you were a massster?"

"He should have seen the Dragon lineage was greater, then," Kirima said.

"Yesss," Shintaro agreed. "He did. That is when he was taken hossstage by the outsiders. They are not ssspirits. They are Volgrians and their lineage is the Phoenix."

"WHAT?" Jai bellowed. "The emperor is in danger?"

Kirima rolled her eyes. "Welcome to the party."

"We have to free him!" Jai insisted. A true zealot of the empire. Had he not been ready to wipe out my men, it would be endearing.

"Where is the helpful information," I asked, tapping my sword to his cheek. "What is this phoenix?"

Shintaro leaned away from my blade. "It is a firebird, much like the Vermillion, but of the Wessst. Their warriors can all use the ability to be insssubstantial for a brief moment. They use that to make it look like there are more of them than there actually are," he said.

"The heirs can also gust wind," I added.

"You will always find the Phoenix clossse to the emperor," Shintaro said. "It's how they keep Massster Kassshvi and Zimo in line. The Phoenix has promisssed the emperor's death if they try to warn the other lineages."

"And what are you getting out of this?" Kirima asked sharply.

Shintaro glanced between us reluctantly admitting, "After Master Feiyu let Ssssan go, the Phoenix promisssed free reign of the dungeons if I finisssshed you both."

"You figured Master Feiyu would let me go. That is why you wanted him to be my challenger." I shook my head at the forethought. I hated to admit it, but he was clever. If it had been used for the betterment of the empire, he might have even been a hero. "And your master?"

"Massster Isssamu is aware of the emperor's predicament, but he did not know of my plans," he defended his master's esteem quickly. It was a lie even Shintaro couldn't sell. Master Isamu was already benefiting from the Phoenix's reign. "That is all I know. Now, let me go."

"You will answer for your treachery when the emperor is free," Kirima said.

"Let me help," Jai pleaded.

I eyed him carefully. I knew he would do anything for the emperor…including kill me, if this all did go to plan and the emperor called for my execution anyway. A smile crept over my face. All the better if the emperor did turn on me; no one could blame me if I took his life for my own.

I unlocked his manacles, saying, "If you want to help, inhabit my fortress, and watch for invaders. This could all be a ploy to bring a greater army to occupy our lands."

"Rhinos break fortresses, remember?" The Rhino master stood, a mountain of a man.

"My troops are trained to move quickly and easily. They can infiltrate the city unnoticed. Yours are…flashy," I said looking at the large, bulky lines of warriors.

"We could use your captain's armor though," Kirima said.

He huffed a complaint, but he knew someone needed to guard the empire's inner border with the Tiger still at rest. He offered two of his pack horses to carry us between the mountains. After an all too short rest, we blazed a trail to the capital.

24

The thick undergrowth snagged the horses' hooves relentlessly. Even worse, the monsoon finally unleashed its floodgates, drenching us to the bone. We had to take an extra wide route around the great lake for fear of the horses sinking in the bog. Even trimming our sleep and pushing the horses to the brink, it took two days to navigate the sharp mountain passages.

"My men are fast, but it will take a week to traverse this ground with two legions on foot," I said, on the final stretch to Caifu.

Kirima's eyes trained on the sodden path. "I can't leave my master in the dungeon that long. Shintaro received word that he is refusing to eat."

"I'm not saying you should. You can report that the Rhino has taken my stronghold," I said and added weakly, "Maybe that will be enough for a provisional release."

"What would I say about you?" she asked, confidence fraying.

I patted my stomach. "The truth—when you scouted the fortress, I was already enacting seppuku."

"What do you think will happen?" she asked heavily.

A silence fell over both of us at the reality we faced. In all likelihood, they would play their cards as if according to the rules of our empire and execute Master Feiyu after a weighted court presentation. The rain began to drown Kirima's poise, wilting her head over her horse like the waterlogged clothes clinging to our skin. I had to offer her some kind of hope, even if it was slight.

"I think… I think they will set a court date and demand fealty to the Phoenix," I said. "That will be our best opportunity to strike." I tugged the horse's reins to climb a mound around a massive, fallen redwood. Its wobbly legs trembled over the soft dirt they now matched in color and texture. As it began to stumble, I kicked my heel into the horse's side, rekindling its will. The horse dug its back hooves into the ground and vaulted to the other side.

She considered, "What if the date is before your men arrive?"

"Then so be it. If the tides turn, Master Isamu will ebb with them." Shintaro made it clear that the Snake was loyal only to itself.

"What of the people in Caifu? They can only withstand so many assaults without losing faith."

"Faith in what? The emperor? Perhaps they should have lost faith in him long ago. Their faith brought them to this," I spat.

"San, you don't mean that."

"I do, Kirima," I insisted. "While we have fought for Xinyue and pillaged lands, the emperor sat on his throne idly. And when trouble did come to his door, he bowed to it. He is nothing more than a spineless man."

She pulled her horse to a quick stop. I slowed and pulled the reins to face her. Our horses puffed and heaved in the downpour. Her intense eyes pierced into mine, defying even a flinch as raindrops pelted her face.

"By the moons, you're serious? Our lives have been dedicated to him. You're a master of one of *his* lineages, Sanav!"

"We are only his lineages so long as we submit ourselves to him."

Her shoulders constricted. "What are you saying?"

"When this is over, I will no longer be one of Emperor Xinya's dogs," I said. She grimaced and turned away. "Master Hito taught me to bow to a force that gives us power. If it exists, it must have lineages even greater than ours. I want to find them."

"What about our people?" she said, eyes as wet as the rest of us. "Your soldiers?"

I shrugged, trying to hide that it took my lungs captive. From the moment Guo tossed me into the pagoda as children, my life had revolved around the Dragon lineage. Instead of killing me for trespassing, Master Hito gave me his signet. I thought about what he taught me every hour of every day until I could show him all I had learned at the Festival of Heirs. The so-called dreadful Dragon master adopted me, and the other lineages accepted me as part of them. If I turned from the emperor, I would lose my family, my friends…

I would lose Kirima.

I sighed, raising my eyes to the relentless sky in a silent plea.

I finally admitted, "I haven't figured everything out yet. Just that I can't keep taking orders from a forgery of power."

She spurred her horse and mine danced to follow. The unending rainfall did little to bolster the dour mood. The horses plodded the rest of the way to the capital, their plopping hooves the only noise louder than the monsoon and my racing thoughts.

"Put on your helmet," Kirima shouted back to me. "Do you remember who you are?"

"Captain Arun of Jai's second legion, sent to accredit your report," I said.

"*Master* Jai."

"Right," I said, reminded that even if we defeated the Phoenix, it had wreaked havoc on our forces and sent our hierarchy into upheaval.

The captain of the emperor's guard met us at the western gate as our horses' heads dipped and wagged with labored breaths. I leaned over and patted mine on the shoulder and brushed its black mane. Dirt caked the cobblestone from the heavy traffic of traders wagering one last haul before the summer monsoons began.

"Hard ride?" he asked on approach.

"The monsoon set in just after we set out," I said, earning a glare from Kirima. "Forgive me for speaking out of turn, Heir."

"It has been a long journey," she said. "Captain Arun came to accredit my report."

"Ah, what news should I send to the emperor?"

I cut in again, "A complete victory. The Dragon captain tried to assault after the second week of siege. We completely wiped them out with minimal casualties of our own."

"The captain?" he asked, "What of the master?"

"He was already enacting seppuku on my first scout of the mountain." Kirima shot a glower at me.

"This is excellent news," the captain beamed. My death was excellent news. I wasn't a hero here anymore. I glanced at Kirima.

"If that is all, we will take our rest in the Leopard's estate," Kirima said. After a few clattered steps, she whispered harshly, "What was that about?"

"What?" I asked, shocked by her sudden spite.

"Why did you talk so much?"

"Have you ever tried to talk to Captain Arun? It's impossible to get a word in!"

She was the one who chose this disguise for me. I would have been just as happy to be Lee, a regular soldier.

She paused thoughtfully. "I don't think I have ever talked to any of the captains."

"What, you stay sequestered in your room all the time?" I asked with a smirk.

"No," she defended. "Until Master Feiyu says I am ready, I watch—I wait."

I chuckled. "You need to take initiative sometimes—learn

from trying. Dare to take the punishment; a few stripes will only add to your belt."

"What a draconic way of looking at things," she muttered.

"You must believe it somewhere in your uptight heart, otherwise you would not have asked for my help," I teased.

"I asked for your help because I thought you were an upstanding imperial citizen," she said bitterly.

"Ah, you're still upset."

Veins bulged in her neck.

"Still upset?" she nearly shouted. Lowering her voice, she whispered, "Did you expect me to get over your treasonous ideas in an hour?"

"Well, no, it's just…"

"Just what?" By the frost in her eyes, I got the sense she was one step from attacking me, but I had no idea why.

"I just don't understand why you're at my throat about it," I said.

"You don't understand? You—you—ugh!" She huffed and kicked her horse into a trot.

I spurred my steed to match her stride. She silently fumed the rest of the ride to her estate in the eastern sector of the city. With the passing of the festival, the visitors had returned to their lives outside the capital, and with the downpouring rain, Caifu's citizens hunkered in their shops and homes striking the streets with a ghostly sense of emptiness.

The courtyard manor was as beautiful in the rain as it was in the sun and moonlight. Bushes edged the outskirts of the manor yard as cherry blossoms dropped pink specks like delicate confetti.

Two servants in fine, lavender silks approached. One took the reins of our horses while the other held a dainty, white umbrella above Kirima's head. Despite the exhaustion we shared, she squared her shoulders and walked like royalty in her estate.

Young warriors lined the stone training platform relentlessly striking wooden dummies until they noticed Kirima enter. They all turned and bowed while we passed the threshold into the beautiful wooden manor. The Leopard had the least numbers in its fighting force, but stories ranked each among the captains in skill. Judging by their flashing qi, the stories did them injustice.

Two warriors appeared in front of the manor doors and hoisted it open allowing us entry. I glanced back as the wood latched into place with no trace of the men. They just…disappeared, but I could sense them watching us.

We turned a corner and were met by an elderly couple. The woman's sleeves covered her hands and extended past her knees. Her dress was complete with all the baubles and frivols that made noblewomen useless in combat.

"Kirima, you're back," the man said.

Hope glistened in the woman's eyes as she asked, "Good news?"

"Lord and Lady Lian, I wish I had more news. The attack was a success. I hope that will be enough," she said. Lord Lian? I had never seen Master Feiyu's parents. I wasn't even aware they were in the capital.

The man's gaze hardened on me. "They have you under house arrest now?"

"Not at all. I came to help," I said.

"Mind yourself, Captain," the man snapped. I turned my eyes to the caramel tiles and glanced to the greenery uniquely maintained inside the home. Vines draped like curtains and flowers sat in hanging pots along the walkway.

"He came to vouch for me," Kirima said. "He is a guest."

Lord Lian's eyes never lost their venom, but his open hostility abated. Deep bags sagged under the couple's reddened eyes.

"Well, come in then, I will have water heated for you both," Lady Lian said.

"Have you heard from the master?" I asked. She caught a breath and flicked an indiscernible look at her husband.

He said, "Feiyu sent a letter a couple of days ago."

"Is he well?" Kirima pried.

"He is deteriorating," the man said. Lady Lian hid her face in her cloth-covered hands as tears streamed down her cheeks. "He said he may not see any of us again."

Kirima turned a pleading look at me. My heart twisted at the thought of the Leopard master emaciated and declining.

"I am certain the Leopard's loyalty has earned counsel with the emperor," I said. All three nodded with a weary hope. The Phoenix wanted the Leopard and the Dragon dead. Most likely, the Tiger would be quietly assassinated after the execution of the Leopard. I wanted to wait on my men to take back the capital, but I feared the consequences of hesitating.

The dragon drifted out of my chest and walked alongside as a servant led me to my residence. I doffed the bulky armor and laid with my eyes to the ceiling.

"It would take much longer than this for Master Feiyu to succumb to starvation," Master Hito tried to encourage.

Starvation? No. The loss of esteem and purpose is what worries me, I thought back.

The dragon drifted above me elegantly. What must it be like to be freed from the weight of this world? "He is more resilient than you give him credit for."

So were you and I once, I thought. *When there is nothing left to take, one's own life becomes very tempting.*

Master Hito breathed, "Seppuku is from my heritage, not his. I am sorry you inherited its ideas."

Don't apologize to me it isn't right, I grumbled and quickly changed the subject. *Is the Giver of Strength from your heritage also?*

He rested at my side thoughtfully. "It was an old story my father told me… It was something about…something about putting breath in our lungs and blood in our veins, but that is all I remember. I was younger than you when the previous Dragon master called on me."

What makes you so sure it is real and not a fable? I asked.

He smiled a toothy, serpentine grin. "Well, the emperor cannot be credited for the air—it extends beyond our borders, and blood flows in Westerners as much as it abides in us. The moon is said to be especially partial to our people, but I have seen much impartiality in our conquests."

I laid in quiet reflection on more than just this mystical power. Kirima would not wait for my troops, and the emperor would want an account of the battle before they arrived anyway. Master

Feiyu's deterioration concerned me further.

I washed quickly and redonned the constricting armor. I nearly knocked into Kirima on my way out of my room. Her hair was smoothly brushed and wrapped in a clean bun. It was as if all of the mud the horses flung onto her had only been in my imagination. How could grime touch such elegance?

"Oh, Heir, I was just going to search you out," I said.

"I am going to sneak in to speak with Master Feiyu."

25

"You are going to *what*?" I snatched her into my room and snapped the door shut.

"They denied my request," Kirima said bitterly.

"And you think this is not a trap?" I asked, skepticism altering my tone.

She huffed, "Trap or not, I won't be spotted."

Kirima paced to the end of the room where bamboo doors stood between us and the outer garden like rods of gold between cloud cover. She turned back to me undeterred by my qualms.

"Kirima, you are not thinking rationally," I said, immediately wishing to recall the words.

"*I* am not thinking rationally?" she blazed. I should have kept my mouth shut. "Says the man disavowing millennia of tradition!"

I bit my tongue, choosing silence though the temptation to bite back was strong.

Millennia of her tradition, not mine. I came from a people at the bottom of Xinyue. Her people could become lords and ladies. I was lucky to hold a broom in Caifu until Master Hito redeemed me.

"You never did care about the higher ways of aristocracy!" She fumed. That was it. I had heard enough.

"The higher ways? That is the most pretentious thing you have ever said." I shook my head in disbelief. She clicked her teeth and grabbed the door handle, inlaid in the plank's edge.

"What is this really about, Kirima?"

The Leopard shrunk in her place like a cat backed into an alley. She bit her lip contemplatively.

"I have never been allowed to talk to anyone outside of my echelon. I've only ever had the one friend, an heir from an untouchable lineage. They warned me you were not nobility at heart, but I told them they were wrong."

"They weren't wrong, but they weren't right either. I care for the order of nobility but not for the frivolity of it," I said. "Even so, there are other lineages to befriend… Baihu isn't so bad." A pretentious prick, but skilled and irritatingly noble.

She shook her head and said, "Each lineage has a role in this empire."

"Yes, I know," I said and listed: "The Dragon expands and defends our borders, the Snake keeps our prisons, the Leopard watches and defends the capital, and so on and so forth."

She shook her head, shoulders concaved. "That is just the surface of our role. We defend the capital, yes, but we do so by managing the lineages."

"Managing the lineages?" I asked, dumbfounded. "You expect me to believe that?"

"Of course *you* wouldn't. No one manages the Dragon because no one has too, but haven't you ever noticed Master Feiyu is always the one mediating? Always the one settling disputes before they even start. Always watching, quietly… That's our— *my* role…"

I set a hand on her shoulder and slowly turned her to face me. Her eyes had never looked lonelier as she bore them through me.

"You are the last person I will ever have an honest conversation with. And I should turn you in, but if I do, I lose you both…"

I placed my other hand on her shoulder and firmly promised, "I will help you free Master Feiyu. As for turning me in, it would be far cleverer to use me for the empire's ends. Wouldn't you say?"

A smile alit and died on her lips. "Master Feiyu will determine that."

"Yes, about that plan to go see him…" I started.

Desperation returned to her face. "I need to see him!"

I knew I could never dissuade her and I would be a hypocrite if I tried. I was as much a slave to my own ambitions for my master.

"Ok, let me get you into the cell."

"How?"

I thought for a moment. Could I really break into the Snake's lair? "That thing you did in your duel with Shintaro where you were in front of him except…not. How long can you do that?"

"The qi mirage? Only a few moments," she said. I had assumed as much. It was an incredible show of qi control for an heir.

"And the imperceptibility?"

She looked out the window with a proud gleam. "I am much better at that."

I paraded down the path to the dungeon with all of Captain Arun's audacity and Kirima at my side. Her eyes were narrow enough to cut through metal, with gripped hands and a taut jawline to match. The monsoon had abated, making for a muggy afternoon, but the first clear one in days.

"This will never work," she whispered.

"It is a better idea than breaking into his cell," I said, waving to the gate guard as we approached.

"Captain Arun, Leopard heir, to what do we owe this pleasure?" the man asked from just within the cave's entrance with folded arms.

A large set of iron bars had been casted at the front of the mine shaft-turned-prison to perfectly fit into the edges. The only way in or out was with the approval of the Snakes guarding their pit.

"We have come to visit Master Feiyu," Kirima said.

He sighed apologetically. "We received word that your request was denied."

"Master Jai wanted the battle relayed to the Leopard master," I added.

"You may enter at your own risk, but the heir may not," he said.

"What risk?" Kirima fumed. "He has gone without food for two weeks!"

"It would seem you underestimate your master more than we do."

"Alright, no need to sour a good day," I said.

The guard stood steadfast. Kirima mimicked his stance. As the two stared each other down at an impasse, I wondered if Kirima would abandon the plan and brute force this, though I couldn't see how. Even Jai would have a hard time trying to break iron bars. I cleared my throat at her. She casted a side eye at me. I flicked my head back toward the path. This armor would be the death of me in a battle. Kirima took a menacing step toward the bars and then turned back down the path.

"She's a joy," the guard spit with a barbed tongue.

"I cannot say I would feel any different if it were Master Jai in that cell," I said.

"Strange lineages," he muttered, unlocking the gate and welcoming me into the dungeon.

It was carved into a rock outcrop that stood not quite high enough to be a mountain. Its use as a mine made it a convenient prison since most miners were working off societal debts. Somehow, the inside felt damper than the air outside. A repetitive dripping sound clicked just out of sight no matter how deep we delved. The further we walked, the thicker the doors became and the more indistinct the moans and cries.

The guard lit a torch to guide our way to Master Feiyu's cell. Three Snake soldiers and a captain sat playing a game of chance on a table just in front of the final outcrop. A black iron door stood as testament to the impossibility of escape.

"What's this?" the captain grunted.

"Captain Arun brings a message to the Leopard from Master Jai, sir."

The greasy-haired captain skulked closer. His eyes creeped across every inch of my armor as he circled. As he left my vision, the hair on the back of my neck zapped alive, triggering my hand into a fist.

The captain laughed, "Calm yourself Captain. We are allies, remember?"

"Just let me into the cell," I snarled uncharacteristically.

"Waspish today, are we?" He grabbed the bottom of one of my armor plates and pulled it into himself. "No manners?"

My hands tensed as I forced them to remain open. This captain was as despicable as Shintaro. The veins in my neck pulsed with lava. Master Hito swirled around me protectively.

"Please. Open the door," I requested sharply.

The captain released my armor with a devilish grin.

"Anything for a comrade," he seethed.

Two guards hefted the door open with a long, echoing creak. The third guard put a torch just inside to light the stygian cave cell.

Master Feiyu's arms hung limply above his head, secured to the wall just high enough to force a permanent kneel. His bony knees were purple with abrasions. Master Feiyu's head hung motionless save for the shallow rise and fall of his chest displacing it.

The torchlight flickered onto innumerable scrapes and bruises. His qi was as dim as the cell.

My ever-present master drifted next to me and softly warned, "Careful, San. If he is as broken as he looks, he will be more dangerous than ever."

"See if you can get him to eat while you're here," the captain said, forcing a bowl of filmy soup into my hands.

As soon as I passed the threshold, the door slammed shut behind me with the heavy clank of a lock. I calmed the welling panic of entrapment with a slow, deep breath.

"What are you doing here?" Master Feiyu rumbled without a hint of movement.

"Master Jai sent me to tell you how your heir turned the battle in our favor," I said loudly, just in case my words could be heard through the door. I knelt in front of him quietly whispering, "Thank you for looking into the emperor."

His head snapped to life, cat eyes training on mine.

"Sanav?" His battered head tilted. "What are you doing here?"

"Kirima wanted to see you." I backed away to make way for the heir materializing.

I stepped back and started shouting a false account of the battle, like a great war tale told to inspire the hearts of men. Kirima dropped to her knees in front of her master, pain painted on her face. She traced her finger on his purple wrists just below the manacles.

He pulled away from her touch. "You both need to leave."

"San agreed to help," she explained.

"With what? Treason?" he retorted beneath my loud proclamations.

"With freeing the emperor."

Master Feiyu shook his head. I didn't want to believe it, but the Snake had broken him. I could see a haunting in his eyes deeper than the darkness in the cell.

"Take my parents and leave. We lost this fight."

"W—we have not yet fought," Kirima stammered.

"Isamu was right, we lost when we sat idly by while the Dragon was forsaken," he admitted with a downcast glower.

Just as my speech ended, metal clanged against the cell door, catching all eyes. Kirima took a breath and disappeared. The door groaned with all the cries of those it had guarded as it was forced open.

"Three masters in one room. Champions of the empire," Master Isamu announced from the doorway, standing over his collapsed captain. "I am surprised you fooled Captain Yan."

"How did you know we were here?" I asked, standing between him and the tamed Leopard.

"Shintaro sent a letter that you agreed to parlay…that couldn't be if you had gutted yourself as Kirima's report said."

I tossed my helmet to the side. Immobilized in armor, this was quite possibly the worst moment for an attack.

"Your heir will only survive if I do," I said, boldly facing the hunched, thin man with beady eyes. "I left him in the Rhino's jurisdiction."

"Young Jai will come around with the emperor's persuasion,"

he said. "Only the Dragon has the gall to disobey when faced with certain death. Even Master Feiyu realizes it is fruitless to fight."

A chill shot through both of us at the same time. Isamu jerked to meet Kirima's attack with a snaking arm around hers. I ripped him into the wall before he could snap her arm. He arched his head back with an enigmatic simper.

"I will kill the Phoenix and free the crown," I stated. "Join me or face the consequences."

"Oh, please," Master Isamu chuckled. "I was the first to challenge the Phoenix, and Master Feiyu will be the last. You tried to claim something beyond you, but she *is* preeminent."

"Yield, Kirima," the Leopard master begged, unable to bring his eyes to ours. "My daughter, please."

"Forgive me, Master, but I will not yield while you are in chains," she declared.

Master Isamu bubbled with laughter. "All three defectors in one cell… I will have whatever I want in this empire. Without the Leopard and Dragon to thwart my every ambition, the Snake will be unstoppable."

"Even if we die, the Tiger will still stand in your way," I curbed, cautiously moving closer.

"The Tiger? Master Kabir is still dormant in the palace and his heir refuses to leave his side."

"Careful, he's slippery," Master Hito warned in my ear.

Cover my pressure points. I slowly slid the tip of my foot to center. Master Isamu snapped his hand to hover between us. His eyes were like deep pits waiting to swallow me in darkness.

My blood boiled thinking about Master Feiyu at the mercy of the Snake's untethered hands.

"Are you confident in that armor?" he baited, sliding to keep Kirima behind me.

I ignored his taunt and stood my ground, daring him to take another step. Any further and he would be in my reach. *There!*

Master Isamu shifted a hair into my range. I swiped an open hand at his eyes, narrowly missing. My gut twisted in horror as I realized his bait. A hand jutted between the plates of my armor, piercing beneath my rib. I shot back before he could grab anything vital, but his pursuit pinned me against the wall.

Kirima dove in with rage. Master Isamu caught her swing with ease, carrying it into a throw while avoiding my hook punch. Kirima slammed into the ground, arching her back in anguish. He quickly jutted back at me with unstoppable speed. My heart hammered as he landed three piercing finger strikes for every one that I blocked. I desperately searched myself, heating my armor with a breath of fire.

Master Hito's voice rang in my head, "Temptation has always been his weakness."

The snake swept a kick through Kirima's arms as she attempted to rise and then he spun a backfist at my face. I dipped as far as the armor would allow, exposing the pressure point behind my head.

Please work, I thought with a quick breath. My hair stood on edge, knowing it was coming. *Just a little longer.*

Like lightning, I arced in the air, catching his death blow as it collided sharply with my throat. Just as I had done to Kirima, I whirled us both in the air, slamming him into the ground with a loud crack.

Only, Master Isamu did not take it lying down. He wrapped an arm around my throat and pulled his legs around my molten armor.

He let out a piercing scream as his legs blistered. I clawed for his eyes with one hand while I struggled with the other to free my airway. I directed the Dragon's qi into my hands. I gripped the arm around my neck, twisting to break the bone except it twisted like mud—slimy and intangible. With a haunting shriek, his elastic limbs clenched tighter and tighter, cutting the air from my lungs and blood from my head. No fire. No grip.

A loud *crack* boomed into the cell.

Kirima had kicked a crater into Master Isamu's head. I sucked in a desperate breath and frantically tore the armor from my skin. Undoubtedly, he had sent word to the palace. They knew we were here. He probably knew we would come the entire time.

"Here!" I said, tossing the keys to Kirima from the Snake captain's body. The other guards were gone—likely with the message of my return. "We have to hurry!"

"You have to leave," Master Feiyu said.

Unbelievable. As soon as we free him, he starts lecturing me.

"I will," I puffed. "Once Master Hito's name is restored."

"You cannot win this, San," he said, wobbling to his feet. "You could not win against Master Isamu, and he could not defeat the Phoenix."

"I was wearing armor," I offered an empty argument. Master Hito could have inspired his confidence, but Master Feiyu still saw me as an heir.

The Leopard master straightened in his tattered robe. "You will not get my heir killed for your vengeance."

"I never asked anyone to help me!" I snapped, sick of his unsolicited admonitions.

"San," Master Hito called with his fatherly hedging. I rolled my head back with an angry groan.

"Master, I asked for his help. We have to do this for the sake of all that is noble," Kirima said softly.

"No," I said, jutting a finger at them both. "This is not for nobility—this is to right the wrong that cost my master's life."

I stormed into the dungeon corridor. Around the bend, the torchlight grew stronger as a squad of guards approached.

They want fire, they will have it. I rounded the corner, spewing flames over the breadth of the dank passage and consuming any guard standing in my way. Screams had never sounded so justified in my ears.

Master Hito watched silently. He didn't have to say anything, but I could see the disapproval in his eyes. I could have spared them, but I hadn't the time to waste on hordes of soldiers. This wasn't a war like the others where we could meet and parlay, and everything would be decided fairly. It started with the shedding of blood, and it would end that way too.

"San, wait!" Kirima yelled, running to catch up.

I kicked past several fallen guards. "You heard your master; you are not permitted to come."

"He relented." She snagged my arm. "This is as much our battle as yours."

"What are you even fighting for?" I stared at the opening ahead.

"For our people. Our empire cannot exist under Volgrian rule, only the emperor's."

I ripped my arm from her grip. "It doesn't make you angry what they did to Master Feiyu? Not just his body, but to his spirit?"

"Of course it does!" she asserted. "He's like a father to me, but the emperor comes before our principles. The emperor is our purpose."

"That's it," I realized. We all broke because of the emperor's failure. Every drop of blood and cry of pain was on his head. He did this to Master Hito, Master Feiyu, Master Rohak, Master Kabir, and me. He's no god; the emperor bleeds.

A stab of pain pierced my head as a primordial hunger flared in my chest. I craved the emperor's blood.

"Don't do this," Master Hito's voice echoed in my mind.

Why not? No one else will put an end to this madness!

The path of the black dragon comes at too great a cost. His voice was coarse and pleading. *The last time a black dragon was born—*

If I must become the monster, so be it. I didn't want to hear the rest of his warning. I knew what the legends said, but how could I be any worse than the charlatan we called a god.

I would see the emperor bleed.

Rainwater poured over the edge of the dungeon's opening like a waterfall over a cliff. I unlocked the gate and pushed it open. Even the waterlogged air felt free in my lungs after walking into the emperor's prison. It felt wrong to leave without the Leopard master, but time was of the essence, and I had a plan. The palace grounds would be easy enough to navigate but someone needed to keep the ghostly warriors out of my hair.

"How did your men turn invisible at the door?"

She wasted a moment deciding whether to divulge their secret. "Why do you ask?"

"Because the Phoenix's men are somehow vanishing, even though they are mere soldiers—Just like yours did."

She gasped, "It's not my men!"

"Sh. I know," I hushed. "It feels different, but how is it possible for soldiers to act as heirs?"

"They are few and so they are trained as rigorously as I am, perhaps even more in some areas. Master Feiyu says that there are those abilities that training unlocks, and others unlocked by direct discipleship of the master."

So, some qi abilities could be trained, and others must be unlocked by mastery…

"Hm, very good. That gives them as good a chance as any against the Phoenix's men. Can you handle that?"

Kirima looked off to the side, "Only if they show themselves."

"When you bring your men against the palace, they will show."

I dropped another unconscious palace guard into the moat. The edges of my vision turned black as my focus tunneled on the Marble Palace. Every lie would be exposed. Every wrong would be righted. The emperor would endure the suffering he had caused out of fear and cowardice. He would meet an agonizing end and his name would become a byword in this empire. I would make it so.

The hunger panged in my chest.

The rain glanced off my jaded skin. Fire burned in my gut and through my soul with each step toward the throne room. I snuck past the maze of bushes, pressed beyond the giant marble columns, and ducked back behind the wall at the sight of a line of palace guards. As little trouble as they posed to me, I refused to risk losing the Phoenix master because of a commotion.

I stripped my eyes from the direct route and stalked to the side of the massive structure. Another guard rounded the corner and opened his mouth in alarm. I cracked the side of his head and heaved him behind a bush. The walls were sheer marble, save for the diamond windows refracting light on the interior, making them impossible to scale. I needed another way.

I had to hurry. Master Kashvi would soon find that Master Isamu was beyond saving and scramble back to the palace. With the sound of two conversational guards about to round the nearside, I was forced to scramble into a tree. I lifted my feet into the cloud of cherry blossoms just as the swordsmen came into view. My heartbeat reverberated through my body like the beating of wings. The men paused under the tree, looking at something on the ground. I squinted to see the indention my foot had made in the softened ground when I jumped to the first branch.

"Someone is here," the guard said, snagging my breath.

As he pulled a horn from his side, I dropped behind them with no chance to think. I grabbed his head and twisted it violently. As soon as I felt the crack, my hand smacked over the other guard's mouth and clenched his cheekbones, strangling his scream. I snapped my other hand into the back of his neck. Both bodies dropped lifeless. The hunger in my chest abated and then swelled in my gut.

"Don't do this; killing the emperor won't satisfy your anger," Master Hito said.

This was all the emperor's fault in the first place. "He took everything from you. How can you defend the cur?"

He exhaled slowly. "I'm not defending him; my concern is for you and your heart."

"My heart is stronger than ever," I whispered, feeling an insatiable burning in my chest.

"A black dragon is unmatched in might, yes. But it is also unmatched in its enduring isolation," he warned. When I ignored him and climbed back into the tree, he tried a different approach. "You've worked so hard to restore our lineage. None of it will amount to anything if you kill the emperor."

I pinched the bridge of my nose. This was not the time. "Even if our name was restored among the people *he* would still claim us. *He* would mar our name by association."

My master hovered around me as I hoisted myself as high into the tree as the branches would allow.

Just like the festival, I thought, before charging over the slick branch. I focused all of my strength into my legs and vaulted at the wall's first ridge. I flew, crashing painfully into the side of the palace. My fingers reached just over the lip and slipped. My nails scraped to the edge of slick marble.

"Allow me," Master Hito said, forcing qi into my hands.

As my hands turned to claws, the marble chipped and relinquished a grip. I clambered up the cascading rims all the way to the top. I looked through the one-way crystal roof and saw my target. The emperor sat on his throne, bouncing his leg impatiently. *Your wish is my command.*

A horn blared in alarm as a palace guard bellowed, "Two guards down! We're under attack!"

That was faster than I expected, but I still had the element of surprise. I plunged through the center like the moonlight, shrouded in the Dragon qi, and surrounded by crystalline shards of glass. The marble floor rippled beneath my feet and shattered with the impact. My eyes shot daggers at the emperor: "You're next."

The emperor leapt to his feet. "What are you doing?"

"This is your fault!" I seethed, bolting at him. The prickling sensation in my gut and chest turned into a stabbing pain. I needed his blood.

A tall woman appeared between us with a hand outstretched to halt me. No chill, no danger. Just like Xael said, it was as if she hadn't existed until that moment. Her robes were a deep red scattered with orange glints, like the embers of a fire, matching her orange hair. Scars marred her luminescent skin as bright red qi wafted from her center. So, this was the Phoenix master.

She stood erect and spoke in halting tones. "This is not expected."

"It should have been."

"All of the other lineages stand and bow at his defense, yet you come to kill your lord. Why?"

"Why do you protect him?" I shot back.

Her hands moved as if conducting her mouth. "It is the smoothest transition of power, since no one defies the lord of this land."

I shook my head. "I have no lord. The Dragon lineage is forsaken."

"Everyone serves something," the woman said, dipping her head to catch my focused eyes. "What is it you serve? We can achieve it together. The Vermillion and the Dragon—just like ancient times. Who would dare stop us?"

Master Hito spoke to me, "That is a flame not our own. Do not indulge in it, Sanav."

"What is it you wish to achieve here, foreigner?" I asked.

She paced thoughtfully, putting together an answer.

I could ensure your name stayed on the hearts of our people forever, I thought to my master.

He flared, "I do not desire infamy."

"You don't know, do you?" she asked.

I glanced between her and the emperor. He shifted uncomfortably. Part of me reveled in his fear. After all he had done, he deserved to fear me.

"Know what?" I asked, eyes caught on the coward emperor, no better than the Westerners.

"He *invited* us," she said. Why would he do that? Our people were ready to lay waste to her lands at the first command. He didn't need to bargain with foreigners to attain their strength, resources, or numbers. "Your emperor is everything you stand against. He feared the Dragon so much that he asked foreigners to find a way to rid the world of you."

Emperor Xinya shrank behind his golden throne. Shintaro said the Phoenix tricked the emperor. Either he lied to me or he had been fooled. One of those seemed far more likely than the other. By the moon, the emperor really made a deal with foreigners. That man—no, that *worm* connived a way to kill my master and end a faithful lineage out of fear and cowardice. How could anyone serve such a gross image of power?

The hunger thrummed again.

"Then why do you stand in my way? He has earned his death."

"I won't stand in your way," she said. Her strained accent slowed her speech. "I only wanted to offer you a place on the throne with me. The firebird and dragon have always risen to the height of kingdoms with unstoppable power. Think of all we could achieve together. All the kingdoms we could claim. All people could be unified."

"I would rather die nameless than have the legacy of a tyrant," the dragon growled.

"Unify under you, Master…?" I prodded.

"Under us," she offered, "Master Sanav of the Dragon and Master Dyoka of the Phoenix."

A commotion started in the hall. Kirima had brought her men too quickly. I glanced to the ornate door, a decision on my hands with no time to consider. Conquer the empire I once served, or free it to return to the emperor's bondage.

Could I even kill this master? She had bested Master Feiyu, something I tried and failed to do. It is said that once a Dragon master gives himself over to vengeance, he loses a piece of his humanity but reaches a new height of power.

"Have you forgotten what she has done to achieve this?" The dragon roared inside my mind. His voice echoed around my skull, rattling my vision. The hunger pangs flared into my head and drowned out Master Hito's voice.

I could run the empire better than that. A snarl curled onto my lips as I watched the crouched emperor knock his knees together. It was time I gave myself over to the hunger for blood.

The doors burst open, revealing Captain Chiyo and Xael. My anger faltered on their ardent eyes. They were weeks early, drenched to the bone, and dripping with blood. Both heaved like horses after battle. They never forsook me. How could I forget them? How easily I could turn into the emperor I despised.

"They are whom I serve," I said, shame dancing in my burning chest.

The hunger exploded in my head, chest, and gut. I stumbled back and gripped my head. The pain raged like an inferno. My hands rattled and I gnashed my teeth trying to get a grip. Master Hito blazed into my mind and roared so loud my vision went black. The hunger fled into the recesses of my mind and everything was clear again.

"You have the same pathetic flaw as your master," the Phoenix master spat, waving her hand for her heirs to come into view.

Lera stepped from behind a golden statue of the previous emperor. She flipped a knife in the air as she joined her brother's side. His golden hair was tied into a tight braid on top of his head with designs shaved into the side. In either hand, a knife danced through his fingers.

Captain Chiyo was a formidable fighter, but two heirs was more than she could handle, and Xael was not yet a fighter. Even more so, two heirs and a master that outmatched the Leopard was beyond me. And yet, it was better to be a dead master than a blood-soaked tyrant.

"Go! I have this."

"Respectfully, not a chance," Captain Chiyo barked back unblinkingly.

The heirs descended on them like birds of prey. I shot to protect my soldiers, but Master Dyoka flew between us. That was the last time she would stand between me and my target. I charged, with my soul alight. I had to get around her. I had to protect my soldiers.

My hands flowed like a raging river, blocking her sweeping blows and countering with pristine accuracy. The Phoenix dropped to the ground, sweeping a leg at mine. I launched over her, soaring like a dragon towards her heirs.

"No!" I screamed, as one ripped off Captain Chiyo's helmet and jumped out of the katana's reach.

I rolled into a sprint across the marble floor. The blond man drove a kick into Xael's sternum, hurling him into the wall. Just as he reared his hand to finish the boy, I spun him by the elbow into my fist. Blood streamed from his lip, but the Phoenix master was upon me before I could finish him. I turned to meet her and heard a haunting cry.

Captain Chiyo gurgled and collapsed, speared through the throat by her own katana. The assassin ripped the sword from Captain Chiyo's neck, splattering her blood across me.

"Sanav, focus!" Master Hito warned, but rage burst through me as I let out a savage roar. Death coursed through my veins and it would be answered.

I catapulted a chaotic fist at the Phoenix master knowing it would never hit. She blocked in a circle and jutted two protruding knuckles into my chest. It cracked and pain stabbed like a dagger had pierced my sternum. I hit the wall and slid to the floor next to Xael.

"Not like this," the dragon demanded.

I kicked off the wall, sliding past her stomp. As I arched off my hands, two more figures tore into the throne room. Kirima and Baihu charged into the fray, forcing the heirs away from the captain and Xael. The Phoenix screeched in indignation as they regrouped.

"What are you doing here?" I asked, wary fists raised and ready to reengage.

"Sorry I was late," Kirima said between breaths. "I thought we might need him."

As much as I hated to admit it, I did need them. My head still rattled from hitting the wall.

"I have fought both heirs, the woman is more dangerous," I said.

"I saw her eyes behind the arrow that struck Master Kabir," Baihu stated. He looked completely healed from our fight. His foot inched toward the battle, eyes glued on his target.

Kirima surveyed the taller heir. "Shall we finish this?"

"You think you stand a chance in this fight?" the master with fire for hair shouted.

"Was that directed at me or your heirs?" I snarked.

The final battle set into motion with our slow convergence. The master's qi surged from her center to her fingertips like lightning running down a tree and dissipating just to strike again. Her spindly hands curled into loose, readied fists.

My chest brimmed with smoke. It itched the back of my throat as it poured out my nostrils. The hatred and anguish boiled inside, searing my knuckles white.

The Phoenix bridged the gap with a low lunge at my gut. I focused qi into my stomach trading the blow for my own across her jaw. Undeterred, two screeching fists circled like vultures toward my forward knee. Instead of taking it away, I jutted it forward, in front of her swing's trajectory. She snagged it to topple me.

"Not a chance," I resolved, as her forearm buckled my knee. I let myself fall back, kicking my leg into her jaw as I went. I landed cleanly, rolling back to my feet.

Sweat dripped down my face, mixing with the rain falling from the gaping hole in the ceiling. I knew better than to hope two hits would fell a master, but exhaustion threatened to take hold.

"Don't allow her to recover," Master Hito advised. I faltered, coughing blood. I struggled even to think. For days, I had traveled without rest and now I faced my second master of the day. I must have been crazy to think I could do this.

"We can do this." The Dragon qi radiated from me like I had never seen. The ghastly aura forced me forward.

The Phoenix master stirred to her feet, hair dangling in front of her face like the crazed monster she was. Time to end this. I filled my chest with a confident breath. Blue fire raged mercilessly at my prey.

"Wow," Master Hito breathed.

She cackled maniacally in the flames. She burst from the inferno with crazed eyes and fiery hair.

My jaw slacked. Her skin was untouched by the heat. All it

had done was alight her heart and tire mine. Kirima screamed at my side, but I hadn't the time to look.

Dyoka tore at me like a banshee. I set a hard block that her hand phased through and crashed into my face. I stumbled, failing to block another fist into my gut. Blood splattered from my mouth. How could I win? My abilities only bolstered this Phoenix. Panic stormed in my mind as a backfist slammed across my face followed by a whipping slap into my ear leaving it ringing like a gong.

"Armor!" The dragon snapped me from my panic. Her fists circled up her center to jab a series of quick strikes at my sternum. I forced my qi into her target, covering it with armored scales. Her wrist and face both twisted.

"My turn." I rippled both hands out like a tidal wave and crashed them into both sides of her head. Predictably, she phased so my hands clapped into each other, but that was not what she should have avoided. I left my hands cupped together as she came back into existence, head next to mine.

"Die, worm!" She screamed with a bladed elbow launching into my ribs.

I waited until her elbow connected, cracking into my unguarded ribs. As my ribs crackled like a dying campfire, I cupped the crown of her head and blazed my qi-charged knee through her face. The Phoenix master stumbled a step back with the force. I shifted the qi into my foot and caved her chest with a single, devastating front kick. She grasped at the empty air with desperate, bloodshot eyes. She mouthed something as blood began spilling onto the floor. We collapsed at the same time.

I hit my knees on the marble, and fell forward onto my hands in a coughing fit. Saliva mixed with blood. My blood. *I should have blocked.*

Master Hito's voice eased my heart like a cool drink of water. "You have done well."

He breathed the last of his qi into me and went dormant. I bowed my head to the cold marble, wrapping my arm around my ribcage. I wasn't ready to die.

"Master San!" Xael shook my shoulder. I toppled to the ground, laying wrinkled like discarded paper. "I don't care what my father says, you're a good leader—you have to live!"

"Move!" Master Kashvi shouted at Xael, barreling over me. She grabbed either side of my chest and white heat flashed through my bones. I writhed in pain as the bones snapped back into compact structures.

"Stop it! You're hurting him!" Xael cried, fighting to get the master away from me.

"Patience," she said. She held one hand out to the boy as she put another on my gut, cauterizing my stomach. I rolled to my knees, ejecting bloody bile onto the slick floor. I dry heaved in agony as she put a hand on my face, reconnecting the jaw with a burst of needlelike stabs. I heaved heavy breaths that craned my back.

"He will be ok."

After a long moment regaining my composure, I looked to the aftermath of the battle. Four corpses contorted on the throne room's floor: Captain Chiyo and three Phoenix foreigners. Kirima stood, holding her crooked arm out to Zimo. Baihu was kneeling with bloodied hands and several scabbed gashes thanks to Zimo's quick work.

"Your men," I said to Kirima. "We need to help them fight the Phoenix's."

"You are far too worn for another battle," Master Kashvi asserted.

Kirima gnashed her teeth as the arm set back straight with a disturbing *pop*. She turned to the entrance, worry creeping into her wincing eyes. "Weary or not, they are mine to lead and protect."

"No need," Master Feiyu said as he entered through the grand doorway. His hair was stringed and greasy like that of a vagrant. Bloodstains, both old and new, coated him from head to toe. "The Phoenixes vanished moments ago. I was worried they came here, but I suppose it is more likely that they fled."

"How could they have known?" Baihu asked.

The Leopard master stared blankly in response. His eyes were dark and downcast as if confined to a darker realm. I shot a look at Kirima. Her eyebrows were creased as she sidled up to him and gently laid a hand on his shoulder. His head jerked up at her touch. He and Master Hito were once unbreakable, or so it had seemed.

The emperor stole my gaze as he appeared from behind his throne.

"Why did you do it?" Emperor Xinya asked with his fist balled as if he had any right to demand an answer.

How dare he speak to me as if he were my lord or master. He should be ashamed of his gutless betrayal of those that had faith in him.

"Do what?" I asked, a savage undercurrent coursing beneath my words.

"This empire could have been yours if you accepted Master Dyoka's offer. Why did you choose to risk your life in its service?" he asked again. The emperor descended from the stairs, looking me in the eyes from an equal standing. How I burned to break his knees—to make him kneel before his lineages.

"My men deserve a better leader than a tyrant," I stated.

His eyes flashed an angry squint. "Is that what I am?"

"You are a fraud," I declared. "You claim to be a god but you are an idle coward."

"Then why serve me?"

"I will not anymore. I intend to find someone greater, or become it," I said. His mouth opened with no words to fill it.

"He is exhausted," Master Kashvi tried to defend my words.

"No," Kirima said softly. Her sad eyes flickered to mine as she approached. "His intent is set, but I ask that you let him leave peacefully for the good he has done."

"What of your men?" the emperor asked.

My chest sank heavily as I thought about them. I was honored to lead them and I once believed no one else in Xinyue could lead them as well as I, but…

"I am not great enough to lead them. My mistakes nearly cost their lives thrice in the month I have been their master." I paused, eyes lingering on Captain Chiyo's blood-soaked body. Her lifeless eyes stared through mine. I breathed, "I did cost my first captain her life."

"What then do you propose," the emperor, untouched by even

a bruise, asked. Baihu moved protectively to his side.

"I will leave. Surely somewhere I can find one who can truly give me power," I said.

"You want me to tell the people the Dragon left to find someone greater than me?" He laughed mirthlessly.

"Tell them the Dragon lineage died defending Xinyue like the Vermillion did in carving Xinyue's place in this world," I said. That would ensure Master Hito's legacy in the hearts of the people and allow the emperor his fraudulent esteem.

"Very well, the name of the Dragon will be restored and honored among my people forever," he declared. I puffed at his arrogance. *His* people? Master Kashvi and Kirima's eyes widened at the emperor's agreement. Baihu watched unmoved, or so it seemed until I caught his toes clutching at the floor.

"You are banished. You have a week to be out of Xinyue before your banishment is made final among the lineages. Kirima, escort him out of Caifu."

I laughed jovially. As if he had the power to stand against me. I would avoid any more quarrels with the other lineages, but not because I feared anyone. With this arrangement the dragon kept its good name among the masses and the emperor could continue his charade. One day, I hoped the other lineages would see it as such and find their own source of power.

"I accept these terms so long as my men are allowed their choice in how to proceed."

"They will be offered the same freedom they have always had to choose," Emperor Xinya said.

"Where will we go?" Xael asked.

We?

His aura flowed in his legs, prepared for a long journey. Truthfully, I had no information to point in any direction, and very few ideas. Perhaps the great Western Coliseum held the great Giver of Power. Wherever I went, it would be dangerous.

"Well, with only a week, I must bury my first captain and be on my way. I pray Master Kabir returns to you quickly," I said sincerely to Baihu.

"I hope you find what you are looking for," he offered back. I smiled at the kindness. Who would have guessed it: Baihu wishing a blasphemer well.

Kirima and Xael walked on either side as I made my leave. I knelt at Captain Chiyo's side, grabbed her hand, and whispered my thanks for breaking through my stubborn vengefulness and for sending me Xael. Xael brought her helmet to me and I placed it over her head. I tossed my rain cowl over my head, hoisted her over my shoulder, and exited the palace for the last time.

I stood over Captain Chiyo's grave the next day, with Xael, Kirima, and Master Feiyu at my side. Master Hito laid a clawed hand on the headstone and bowed his head. He would only be able to stay out for a short time. Our qi was still weak from the battle and the separation strained us both.

Kirima and Xael looked to me to start the send-off ritual. What words could honor her service as much as she deserved?

"To the captain who proved to be the most faithful of all," I said.

"To the captain who fostered me," Xael voiced.

"To the captain who saved Xinyue," Kirima resounded.

Master Feiyu quietly concluded, "Three cheers to a captain worth a thousand more."

If anyone deserved the honor of a three-pronged hail, it was Chiyo, first captain of the Dragon.

She would have made a good heir, I silently shared with the ethereal dragon hunkered over her grave.

"Yes, she would have," he admitted. "But she was a far better captain. No one could have tended to the soldiers better and no one would have enjoyed it more."

An eagle screeched from the sky. Master Feiyu held out his arm for the eagle to land. Worn qi protected his forearm from the sharp talons. He plucked the knot around its leg and unraveled the note. Though not a part of this empire any longer, curiosity pricked me. I raised an eyebrow.

He sighed, "Master Jai sends his gratitude for ending the Phoenix, and his apology. Shintaro gained mastery and escaped his confinement last night."

"Hm," I said, mulling over the places he might go. Ultimately, he was now the empire's problem, not mine. "I suppose you will have some hunting to do."

The Leopard master stared blankly until Kirima snapped him from whatever place took his mind captive.

"Yes," he agreed as if there had been no pause. "I need to send a few more messages. Kirima, meet me at the manor after you escort them from the city."

He turned and hastened onto the open streets.

"Will he be okay?" I asked Kirima. She nodded, although her eyes trailed after him.

"Will *you* be okay?" I asked, placing a hand on her shoulder.

As her master faded into the distance, she turned back to me. "We will be fine. What of you? It is a long journey out of Xinyue."

"Don't worry about us. I hear Xael is an excellent pack mule," I joked, nudging him with my elbow. "Maybe he'll even carry me part of the way."

"I bartered for our supplies and packed our bags last night, but I still don't know where we're going. Should I have bought rock-climbing equipment? Snowshoes? Disguises?"

He had spent all morning complaining that I wouldn't tell him where we were going. The truth was, I didn't know where to go. My whole life was wrapped up in Xinyue's glory. There was not a kingdom in the world I believed to be greater than this empire nor a lineage greater than mine.

"My mother was from the same island as Master Hito," Kirima muttered. "She used to tell me stories of a lineage even greater than the Dragon—the Komainu. If you don't have anywhere to go, you could start there."

I snapped a quizzical look to her. "You never mentioned this before."

She sighed, "I hoped you would change your mind…but

I should have known. You've never backed away from your heart's intent."

I swallowed, wishing I could fulfill both of our desires and yet knowing I couldn't. "Well, where is it? I would like to meet this master."

She blinked rain from her eyes. "She said the lineage disappeared shortly before Xinyue's foundation. I know it is of little aid, but perhaps it offers a place to begin."

"Great!" Xael shouted. After a moment he added, "We'll head…where?"

"Hm, the Honin province," I muttered, biting my cheek "That would still be inside Xinyue."

"I won't tell if you don't," she smiled knowingly.

I grabbed Xael's scruffy hair and asked, "Don't you tire of the near-death experiences?"

He grinned brightly. "Are you kidding? I live for it!"

"Your masochism is as inspiring as it is frightening," I chuckled.

At the edge of the capital, Kirima grabbed my arm. Her eyelashes batted back tears. "San, keep yourself safe out there."

I raised my hand to her cheek. She was the hardest thing to leave behind. I had shared the brightest and deepest moments with her…but we were on irreconcilable paths, and I wouldn't ask her to wait on me.

I softly tipped the bottom of her chin and said, "Talk to some commoners for me… Make a friend here."

Kirima nodded gently. I dragged my feet to leave. Even my homeland was part of this empire now. It would take time to rebuild the lineages, but soon Baihu would lead the assault on the West, claiming more and more land as part of Xinyue, and I would be welcome in none of it.

I looked to the sky, wishing for an easier direction. Even if one existed, would I take it?

My feet finally relinquished their implantation and set off on the western road. I would need to make it look as if I left the empire before turning back to my master's homeland. I always wanted to visit the Honin province.

I had lived through being conquered, captured, elevated, and exiled. I had secured the era of the Dragon as its champion heir and brought it to its end in a greater quest for knowledge and power. Certainly, none could say they had lived a more colorful life than I, and I had only just begun.

Epilogue

"Lace the jib with the line!" The helmsman, Captain Kuki, called from the prow where he tended to the wooden figurehead.

"Do what to what with what?" I shouted over the howling wind coming from the seas. A storm was on the move and it would set back our work for at least a day once it hit. Xael bounced an equally bemused expression between us.

The captain bellowed a hearty laugh that could be heard for miles from port. The wind whipped his wispy white hair toward the sea. "They wasn't kiddin' when they said yer a couple land lubbers. Say, how'd the two o' ya find yerselves out on these stretches?"

"He's the—" Xael started but I cut him off.

"We were in the Dragon lineage and thought we would do some searching before joining another legion." The ship rocked against the ropes tying it to the dock.

It had been years since I lived an anonymous life. No one

waited on me; no one gained from doing me any favors. It was a quiet existence I hadn't realized I missed. Of course, Xael wanted to tell everyone of my accomplishments at every turn. Sometimes I think he forgot we were exiles. Keeping him quiet was almost more work than upkeeping a forsaken lineage's status. Almost.

"Well, I can't be payin' ya for nothin'. Yer goanna hafta pick up the mariner jargon and help sail The Lotus Moon properly," he said.

"The Lotus Moon?" Xael asked me. I shrugged. The ship's name made as much sense as most of the man's sentences.

"Oh, no…" Captain Kuki grumbled looking down the pier. A few thugs strutted down the boardwalk like they owned the world, or at least this tiny slice of it. "Go on and breathe in the turnin' seas'n. I'll pay ya both on the morrow."

"If they intend to cause you trouble, we can stay. As I said, we were soldiers," I offered.

"Without weapons? They've each got a host o' shivs the size o' yer thighs." He waved us off. "Now go on."

Xael and I slipped into the storage building across from the ship. He was an odd old man, but the captain had been only good to us in the short days we had known him. The empire could use more good-hearted men like the captain. Especially with Shintaro back on the loose. We—the empire was lucky he snuck away quietly.

"Old man, it's time you caved," the goons' leader said.

"I won't be takin' none of yer goods nowhere," the captain stated firmly. "I pay my fees and tha's all."

"You'll carry our cargo, or you'll end up like that kid o'

yours… Did they ever find him?" The man taunted, tapping the flat of a serrated dagger against the captain's bicep.

"Yer goods kill people," Captain Kuki said with a shaky voice.

"Better those you don't know than those you do," the scraggly thug said. The captain quaked in his weatherworn boots. He had seen his share of trouble at sea by the looks of them, but his stance was weak on solid ground. He quivered in the cutting wind.

"What'll it be?"

I felt my fingers around the grainy, wooden door, ready to defend the old man. Xael and I came to this port on rumors that a power protected it from pirate raids. So far, all I saw were people pretending to be more important than they were. Xael and I saw a lot of that recently.

"Komainu help me…" Captain Kuki bemoaned, wagging his sorrowful head. My eyes lit with recognition. That was the lineage Kirima mentioned. Two years of rundown bars and old mining town myths led me here—to Captain Kuki. These thugs should have picked a different old man. Master Hito's turquoise qi flashed in my eyes as I threw the door open. The captain was under my protection now.

Acknowledgments

I don't want to start my acknowledgements with a boring meta-analysis summary…but let's just say gratitude is an underrated psychological resource these days. So, take a moment to share in my abundant gratitude.

To you—my reader—thank you for being part of Sanav's journey. I wrote this for you. I've prayed for you, that this story resonates in your heart and offers you hope. Your life is valuable beyond measure, and I am forever grateful that you invited my story into your internal world.

To my family, thank you for exemplifying the courage seen in these pages. You've sacrificed for your dreams and mine. I couldn't possibly thank each of you enough here but know that I've witnessed a strength in your hearts that has inspired me through many long nights.

To Abigail, my editor and friend, thank you for doing the hard work of "chiropractoring" this story into shape. It would be brittle, bare bones without you. Your son is a lucky boy to have such an amazing mother.

To my dear friend, Alli Prince, thank you for answering five thousand publishing questions and encouraging me every step of the way. I proceed with this book in the wake of your courage.

To Shihan White, my sensei, thank you for being hard on me! You bring levity and humor into the dojo, but you never let that lead to slacking or sloppy training. You've always met me where I was, pushed me to grow, and celebrated my progress. Without you, this book wouldn't exist.

To my dad, I have seen more strength and perseverance in you than in anyone else, fictional or real. You led me spiritually so I didn't have to search for the one true God like Sanav did in this story, and you showed me all the ways I can rest in the Lord's embrace.

To my husband, Sam, thank you for showing me strength in a way I had never seen before. Your gentleness and patience speak volumes about your steadfast courage. If not for your support throughout this process, Scion of the Dragon would be a daydream or a forgotten document in the catacombs of WIPs.

To my mom…she can't read these words, but one day I hope to read them to her. Thank you for giving me this life that I love and pointing me to an eternity I will love even more. Your dauntless, selfless love is the thing of legends. Anyone touched by this story has been touched by you. We all owe you our thanks and the Lord our gratitude for giving you to us for a time.

C.K. Slorra

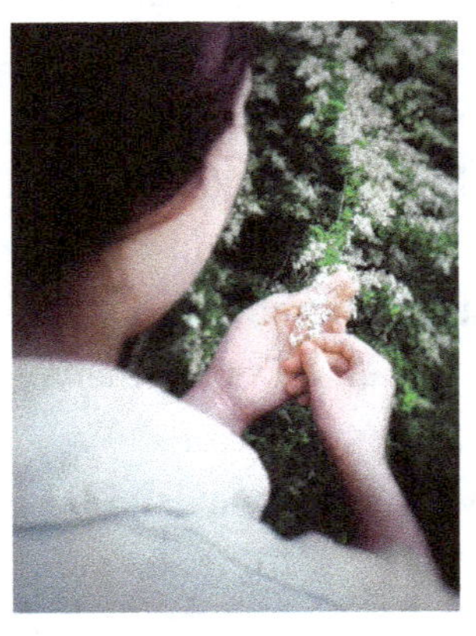

C.K. Slorra is an eclectic author who combines her fervor for martial arts, psychology, and fantasy into riveting tales. When she's not crafting exhilarating YA Action Fantasy, you can find her exploring the countryside with her husband, Sam, and their three spirited dogs. C.K. is on a mission to revolutionize the genre, delivering stories that go beyond mere clichés or erotica, offering readers profound truths, harrowing tales, and pulse-pounding fight scenes that leap off the page.

Help other readers find books that they'll love by leaving an honest review of this book at Amazon.com or Goodreads.com

www.ingramcontent.com/pod-product-compliance
Lightning Source LLC
Chambersburg PA
CBHW070457300726
48975CB00007B/2212